NIPPON ABOOT

NIPPON ABOOT

James Barclay

LINDSAY PUBLICATIONS

First published in 2002 by
Lindsay Publications
Glasgow

© James Barclay 2002

ISBN 1 898169 28 4

The moral right of the author has been reserved

British Library Cataloguing-in-Publication Data
A Catalogue record of this book is available
from the British Library

Designed and typeset by Eric Mitchell, Bishopbriggs, Glasgow
in Plantin 10 on 12 point
Cover illustration by John Gahagan, Glasgow

Printed and bound in Finland by WS Bookwell

CONTENTS

DEDICATION

*To Alex – my brother-in-law – who
appreciates a good Nip*

CHAPTER ONE

SADIE HUNTER LOOKED AT THE FIGURE RELAXING IN THE EASY-chair reading his *Evening Times* and shook her head with a sigh of one who is in deep despair.

Erchie, her spouse, did not look up. He did not notice the look of disdain on his wife's face.

"Ah hope that's the Situations Vacant column you're lookin' at," Sadie snapped.

Erchie grunted. "Ye know fine well that Ah canny go back tae work because of ma lumbar problem," he replied without looking up.

"Erchie, the only lumber connection you've got is me. Ah'm the only wan ye could pick up at Barraland and Ah've been lumbered wi' ye ever since," Sadie said snidely.

"Ur you suggestin' that Ah couldnae hiv attracted the attention of any young, attractive lassie in the hall that night?" Erchie said a little hurt.

"Erchie, you couldnae hiv attracted the attention of any ugly *auld* wumman that night. Come tae think o' it ye could'nae have caught the eye of any auld *man*."

"Ah attracted *you* didn't Ah?" her husband replied with a smug expression.

"That wis because Ah had somethin' in ma eye that night," Sadie replied.

"Ah know ye had . . . *me*," Erchie chuckled.

"Ah, you were a different man then," Sadie said. "Ye wore an air . . ."

"An air o' confidence?" Erchie was thinking back to his youth.

"Naw, an 'air piece oan yer heid," Sadie corrected. "An' teeth as well."

"Ur you suggestin' that Ah'm getting auld?" Erchie moaned.

"Ye wur always auld, Erchie," Sadie said. "Ye wur the only wean in the street wi' grey hair."

Erchie squirmed. "That's a lie," he snapped, "Ah wis blond . . . Ah had a Scandanavian look."

"Scandalous look, aye, Scandanavian look, naw," Sadie said. "It wisnae jist yer grey hair, Erchie. Ye was always auld. Mind the time ye went intae the Post Oaffice for tae buy a stamp and came oot wi' a bus pass?"

"So, whit's wrang wi' that?"

"Ye wur only ten Erchie. While the other weans played wi' their girds you played wi' yer zimmer."

Erchie angrily threw his newspaper on the floor. Sadie had been riling him since he lost his job at the Shakuti factory near their Glasgow east-end tenement home.

"Dae you think ah like bein' idle?" he snapped. "Dae you think Ah *like* bein' oan the dole, eh?"

"Naw, Ah *know* ye don't like hivin' for tae go doon tae the broo, Erchie," Sadie said. "Ye *love* it."

"That's rubbish," Erchie retorted.

"Tae maist people goin' tae the broo is a come down. But no' tae you. You feel important. Ye're the only wan wi' his ain cubicle. Yer name's above it on a brass plate. Erchie, ye've been goin' there that long the commissionaire opens the door and salutes ye every time ye turn up." Sadie was on her high horse.

Erchie beamed. "Ah'm oan first name terms wi' him," he said proudly.

"Erchie, you're oan first name terms wi' the Minister," Sadie snapped.

"Everybody's oan first name terms wi' the minister," Erchie grumbled.

"No' the Minister for Social Security, they're no'," Sadie retorted.

"Well, Wullie the doorman at the broo is a nice bloke," Erchie said. "Ah appreciate him salutin' me when Ah go in."

Sadie threw up her arms.

"Erchie, he thinks you're the bloody manager," she cried.

Erchie ignored his wife's snide remarks. Wullie the broo's doorman was once one of its best customers who had been signing on at that very establishment looking for work as a bouncer. But local clubs had already signed up all available bouncers mostly from former Salvation Army men and women who had lost their vocations. Most of their muscle-experience was learned by ejecting protesting tramps from the *Love and Mercy* Mission hall.

When the tramps, tongues hanging out, invaded the dole office looking for help and were refused it – mostly because they were not asylum seekers from another impoverished country – they started shouting and kicking up a racket. Some even used bad language —

Wullie, who just happened to be signing on that day when the commotion started, immediately jumped into action. He felt sorry for that ragged, filthy starving army of tramps who just wanted some love and something to eat. It was with a tear in his eye that he grabbed them one-by-one by the scruff of the neck and shoved them through the swing doors without first opening them. He chucked them out with a flea in their ear. But that didn't matter to Wullie. One more flea made no difference. As Wullie turned to sign-on he was given a standing ovation by the appreciative staff and, instead of signing-on he was signed up on the spot to become the official doorman. He was always polite with Erchie who slipped him at least two good sized dowts in his outstretched hand – usually Benson and Hedges. Erchie clicked his teeth which he had remembered to put in that morning and winked at Sadie.

"Wan o' these days, hen," he said, "Ah'll surprise ye. You'll see." Erchie's sudden show of confidence was lost on Sadie.

"Erchie," she said, "ye're wastin' yer time. Ye'll never get a joab doon there. Yer appearance is against ye for a start."

"Is that so?" Erchie said angrily. "Let me tell you that only last week they oaffered me a joab. They said they was gien' me a chance and hoped that Ah would throw masel' intae ma new employment."

"Whit was the joab?" Sadie asked, her brows rising.

"Grave digger at Dalbeth Cemetery," Erchie said, puffing out his chest.

Sadie laughed. "Ah see noo whit they meant when they telt ye tae throw yersel' in tae yer work. Aw, Erchie, ye're an awfu' man, so ye ur," Sadie gave her husband a playful dig in the ribs. For all Erchie's faults and her nagging him, she still had feelings for him. It would not stop her nagging him to find a job. She was furious when he lost his employment at the Shakuti factory.

"How did ye no' take the joab?" she asked.

"Ye know coaffins gie me the creeps. Ever since Ah saw

9

Dracula Ah could never look at another coaffin."

"Leave yer maw oot o' it. A joab's a joab," said Sadie facetiously. "Ye had a good joab in Shakuti's."

Erchie ignored the mention of his mother.

"You ur a racist, that's your trouble," Sadie added. "That's the reason ye couldnae settle intae workin' at Shakutis, so it is."

"Ah am nut a racist," Erchie retorted." Ah hiv *never*, ever, been a racist. Gie me wan instant when racism ever entered ma mooth or ma actions."

"Ye'll no' go tae Blackpool," Sadie snapped.

"A loat o' folk don't go tae Blackpool. That disnae make them racist," Erchie answered.

"Whit aboot oor Aggie's wedddin'?" Sadie went on.

"Whit aboot it?" Erchie said, brows furrowed.

"Ye got up and sang *That Old* White *Magic*."

"Ye forget Ah'm colour blind," Erchie said.

"Don't gie me that," Sadie retorted. "You ur a racist and are un-politically correct. In fact ye're no' correct in anythin'."

"Listen tae Mother Teresa," Erchie snapped. "You ur as much a racist as ye say Ah am."

"Oh, an' whit makes ye think that?"

"Well . . . er . . . well . . . erm . . ." Erchie stammered.

"Jist gie me wan instance," Sadie said.

"Well . . . er . . ." Erchie's eyes suddenly brightened. "Ye'll no' eat black puddin'," he said with a note of triumph.

"Ah do nut like black puddin' or white puddin'," Sadie cried. "Ah'm surprised Ah even allow *you* in the hoose. You ur the biggest puddin' Ah know."

Erchie went silent for a while. All this conflict just because he got fired from Shakutis. He was glad that he hadn't been fired from a 'proper' job like a brain surgeon or something.

Erchie had never liked the idea of working for a Japanese firm. As for political correctness, he thought that was a term used by the prime minister knowing what spoon to use when the table was laid and the soup came round. He had gone to see the film *The Seven Samurai* thinking it was something to do with Snow White. Although the Samurai were warrior saviours, Erchie only saw them as a bunch of hard men. He did not like anything Japanese after that. Sadie's voice invaded his thoughts.

"Aye," she said with a sneer, "ye had a good joab an' ye blew it."

"Ah jist don't like the nips," Erchie said his lip curling. Sadie threw up her arms.

"Listen tae him!" she cried, "Don't like the nips, he says. If Dracula attacked you he'd become an alcoholic. Ye've got mair nips in ye than ye'd find in a Tokyo phone book – don't like the nips – huh!" Sadie spat out the word.

"You know whit Ah mean," Erchie said, "Ah'm no' talkin' aboot them real Scottish nips of whit you ur referrin'. Ah am talkin' aboot them nips that John Wayne took on in the *Flyin' Seabees* an' that."

"Ach ye're talkin' rubbish. Ye got fired frae a good joab an' that's that."

"Listen," Erchie said. "You don't know whit it was like workin' in that factory. It was slave labour. We jist didnae see eye-tae-eye right frae the day Ah started. Well, they wee Japs were a loat weer than me for a start, especially that wee Jap gaffer. He jist took a scunner tae me frae the first day he saw me."

Sadie's eyes looked towards heaven. "So why should he be any different frae the rest o' us?" she said.

Erchie let Sadie's snide remark pass. "Ah am dead against these Japs and Jerries comin' here and employing *US* . . . the *VICTORS*. We hiv become the servants. Ah am nut in favour of this Common Market that we ur in and Ah telt that wee Jap gaffer that."

"An' whit did he say tae that?" Sadie raised her brows.

Erchie gazed at the ground and shuffled his feet. "He says that Ah should be glad we're in the Common Market and that Ah should do well in it because he'd never met anybody mair common than me."

Sadie stifled a giggle. Erchie knew that Sadie didn't mean any of the facetious remarks she had made to him. It was love at second sight with him. The first time he met Sadie she didn't have her teeth in. Things were tough in those days. Erchie was a bit of a hard man and had a reputation as a man not to be tangled with. He remembered that first night he had strolled into Barrowland. The band – Billy Macgregor and the Gaybirds – immediately stopped playing and went on strike. Sadie tried not to smile. Not at the striking situation but because she didn't have her teeth in. But for that she was attractive. Her beautiful pink crinoline dress matched her gums. That was the night that Erchie hadn't noticed her. But he *did* notice her the next night when he asked her to dance. The band's strike had been settled with a promise that free bags of whelks would be available at the interval from the seafood shop next door to the ballroom. Free pins to exract the said whelks would be given out. Everything had gone well and Erchie escorted her home that night. He had managed to get a couple of bags of whelks from a trombone player and, as Erchie and Sadie stood at the back of the close, they attacked the delicacy.

"How about you comin' oot o' yer shell as well?" he whispered to Sadie, whose mouth was crammed with rubbery whelks.

Sadie spat some out. "You ur very fishy minded. Maist fellas gie lassies boaxes of chocolates – no' bags o' wulks. Ah should've known there was somethin' fishy aboot you."

"Whit dae ye mean?" Erchie said, putting his hand to his heart.

"Ye've got mair haun's than an octopus. Ye jist don't know where tae put them, dae ye?"

"Ah don't know whit ye mean," Erchie protested.

"Grabbin' a lassie's buttocks when ye're dancin' is nut gentlemanly," Sadie said.

"Ah never grabbed yer buttocks while we was dancin," Erchie cried.

"Naw, no' mine. When we was daein that tango you wur grabbin' that big blonde's erse every time we got close."

"Aw, how could ye think that, Sadie," Erchie said. "Ah was intoxicated by your beauty."

"Intoxicated, aye," Sadie said, screwing up her nose.

Erchie and Sadie were winchers after that despite Sadie's abhorrence of whelks. Erchie got the message and replaced the whelks with soor plooms. It was Sadie's father, Jake, who almost scuppered the romance. Jake, real name Clarence, had changed his name to that of his favourite drink. He wanted something better for his only daughter. Erchie, to him, was a waster.

But as time went on Jake changed his mind. It happened suddenly when Sadie brought Erchie home one night after a night at the Geggie. Erchie had brought Jake in a bottle of Eldorado and they suddenly became blood brothers.

Erchie had mellowed as his courtship progressed. Sadie had managed to keep him in line and even talked him into finding work. He thought he'd try and find employment with something close to his heart and, being an animal lover, got a job as a butcher.

It was the era of the Teddy Boys when Erchie proposed. Sadie was delighted and, with the aid of a Prudential cheque, invaded Marks and Spencer and C & A's, in Sauchiehall Street, for her wedding outfit. She wanted something more modern than the traditional white wedding gown and veil. Some people said that she should have purchased a thick veil . . . for Erchie.

Everybody agreed that Sadie was beautiful as she marched down the aisle on the arm of her father. Folk did not recognise Jake as he was sober and had shaved. But there were gasps when Erchie arrived at the church. Sadie had arrived first and was waiting, foot tapping, for her fiancé to arrive. She had warned him that he was to discard his boiler suit and show up in something modern and *not* in the tile hat and tails he had suggested. A Teddy-boy suit would be the height of fashion, she said. Erchie had scoured The Barras and Paddy's Market for suitable apparel and had found a brown gaberdine suit with velvet collar. He bought it with his savings of two pounds and proudly took it home. It was only then he discovered the velvet collar was really grease engrained in the material. And the fact that it would have fitted Oliver Hardy didn't matter. He wouldn't have time to have it altered and, on the wedding day, stood at the foot of the aisle awaiting his bride, padded with cushions.

Sadie was shocked.

Sadie's mother began to question Erchie's state of mind But Sadie tolerated his practical jokes. She was just glad he hadn't turned up in a Mickey Mouse suit. They got on well and despite Sadie's protests at him losing his job at Shakuti's, there was still that affection that blossomed all those years ago at Barraland. Erchie felt sour over it. But he reckoned that he was a born loser. In this world, he supposed, there were leaders and followers, winners and losers. He just happened to be a loser. He was once mugged after cashing his Giro cheque. He wasn't surprised. He *was* surprised when the police arrested his mugger who was his mother.

He had left his butchering job when Sadie told him she was becoming a vegan. It took her a while to calm him down when he blew his top protesting that he was, under no circumstances, going through their married life celibate. He was relieved when Sadie explained what the term meant. For now they had a beautiful daughter, Bunty, the apple of her daddy's eye.

Sadie was worried. With Erchie losing his job and Bunty starting winching she could see wedding bells looming. For Bunty had never been so enthusiastic over an affair before. They still had to meet Bunty's intended but Sadie knew what was causing Bunty's heart to flutter so much.

Erchie had begun to read his paper again. "He's too comfortable," Sadie thought. She wondered what her tactics should be to get her man back to work. He would never plead for his old job back, that's for sure. His pride would never allow that. There had to be another way.

"Erchie," she began, "*The Bridge On the River Kwai* wis jist a picture . . . a film. Ye canny let that ruin yer life."

"Whit makes ye think that's whit influenced me?" he said.

"Erchie, pictures dae influence *you*," Sadie said flatly. "Mind the time ye went tae see *The Sound of Music*? No' only did ye hate the Nazis for the wey they treated the Wan Trap family, ye wanted me for tae become a nun. Aye, pictures definitely influence *you*. In fact ye're oaften under the influence."

Erchie scoffed at Sadie's outburst. "Ye're talkin' tripe," he said. "Ah saw *The Desert Song* six times an' it disnae affect me."

"Ye smoke nuthin' but Camel," Sadie chided. "Tell me, whit got ye in the bad books at Shakis?"

"How should Ah know?" Erchie shrugged. "A' Ah said tae that wee gaffer was, 'Hello China' an' he nearly went through the roof."

"Well, it's like me sayin' tae you 'Hello Taffy', you widnae like that. Ah mean the Japs an' the Chinese were at war wance." Sadie knew her history.

"Ach, Ah was gettin' naewhere in that corporation," Erchie said. "It was a slave camp. An', besides, Ah am against they Jerries an' Japs buildin' their factories here . . . takin' up good spaces that could be used for mair important things whit are mair in line wi' oor culture . . . like steamies an' bingo halls an' things."

14

"Erchie, ye must admit that the Germans and the Japanese hiv brought a lot o' work here. They gie a loat o' work tae a loat o' people." Sadie was on her high horse.

Erchie grimaced. "Naw, naw," he said gruffly, "you jist don't understaun'. That factory was run like a prison camp. That bloody wee gaffer struts aboot wearin' a Royal Stewart kilt. There was talk aboot them chingin' the name tae McTavish's. Ah would've done them under the Trades Description Act, so Ah wid've."

"Ah could do *you* under the Trades Description Act," Sadie said. "Pretending ye're a husband and workin' man. Naw, Ah canny say anythin' bad aboot they Japanese comin' here. Look at Silicon Glen."

"So, they make false boobs . . . so what?" Erchie sneered.

"It's nuthin' tae dae wi' false chests," Sadie said. "They make chips an' things. for computers. They ur very clever."

"Well, tha wee gaffer might think he's a Scotsman but he's no'. An' Ah'll tell ye this," Erchie said, angrily. "That is nut a dirk he has stuck doon his soack. It is a Samurai sword."

"Ach, ye're haverin'," Sadie said with a dismissive wave.

"Haverin'?" Erchie cried, "Haverin', am Ah," he repeated. "Listen, ye're just workin' away there quite the thing mindin' yer ain business when this wee nyaff swaggers up an' says sarcastically, 'Hey you . . . you no' workin' velly good, so you no' . . . cheeky swine."

"That's fair enough if ye're shirkin," Sadie said.

"He didnae hiv for tae belt ye ower the heid wi' his sword, so he disnae," Erchie snapped. "That was definitely a Nippon factory, so it was."

Sadie nodded in agreement. "Ah know," she said cynically, "youse wur always nippin' oot tae the pub so youse wur."

Erchie resented the snide remark. "*Nippin' oot tae the pub!*", he cried, "Listen, hen, ye couldnae even leave yer bench for a minute or youse were on breid an' watter in the canteen for a foartnight. If ye hud for tae leave yer bench for any reason, ye had tae turn an' bow. If ye didnae bow ye'd had it." Erchie spoke bitterly.

Sadie pooh-poohed his remarks. "Ye're talkin' gibberish so ye ur," she sniped.

"Gibberish is it?" Erchie cried, slapping his newspaper hard on

15

the table top. "Look whit happened tae Wee Gumsy McFarlane. He left his bench an' went up tae that wee gaffer an' said politely, 'Can me go for El Crapo – sez-vouz-plez.' But he made the big mistake. He forgot tae bow."

"So, he broke the rules," Sadie sneered. "Ah suppose he got put on breid an' watter for a foartnight?"

"He was immediately sent tae the Okinawa branch," Erchie snapped.

"That was gaun a bit faur was it no'?" Sadie said.

"It was when ye were dyin' for a crap," Erchie said.

"Ach, Ah don't believe wan word o' a' this," Sadie said dismissively.

"You don't know the hauf o' it, Sadie," Erchie said, shaking his head. "There was nae union tae back ye up. An' there was nae promotions. Nut wan Glesca bloke was promoted while Ah was there."

"That was all o' six weeks," Sadie interrupted sarcastically.

Erchie did not respond. "Only their ain wur promoted. We a' did the menial tasks – except Wee Shuggie McShooders."

"Wee Shuggie got *promoted*?" Sadie said, raising her eyebrows. She knew Shuggie who, she reckoned, was as thick as two planks. She remembered when Shuggie's old mother died how he went round the undertakers looking for a funeral director who was offering one coffin and get one free.

"He took jaundice and was made a gaffer," Erchie said bitterly.

Sadie threw up her hands in despair. "Whit total nonsense," she cried, knowing that he was trying to justify his sacking.

"It's the God's honest truth Ah'm tellin' ye," Erchie said raising his voice. "And that's another thing – they don't believe in God. Ye'll never guess whit they worship?" Erchie had a smug expression.

"Tell me," Sadie said, drawing down her brows.

"Widdin poles," Erchie said, pleased with himself.

"*Widdin poles*?" Sadie cried out loudly.

"Aye. Widdin' poles," Erchie repeated. "Or for to be more precise – hockey sticks."

Erchie felt smug and pleased that he had imparted knowledge to his spouse previously unknown to her. *He* was the master in his own house – if not at Shakutis.

16

"Whit are ye talkin' aboot Erchie?" Sadie was tiring of this uninteresting conversation.

"Ah'm tellin' ye the truth," Erchie was adamant, "Ah wance asked that wee nyaff whit religion he was – if he was a catholic or a protestant – know whit Ah mean?"

Sadie didn't answer. She stifled a yawn.

"You'll never guess whit he said they *worshipped*," he went on.

"Do tell," Sadie said bringing her hand up to her mouth.

"*Shinty*," Erchie said with a flourish.

"*Whit?*" Sadie cried.

"Ah couldnae believe it masel'," Erchie said incredulously. "Ah know some folk make sport o' their religion but . . ."

"Ye can say that again," Sadie said. "You look on Ibrox Park like Muslims look on Mecca. An' Big Brendan O'Brien doon the street looks on Parkheid like it was Lourdes."

"Aye, he's always lookin' for a miracle there," Erchie interrupted sarcastically.

Sadie let it go.

"Imagine makin' sport yer religion," Erchie said, shaking his head. "Especially shinty."

"It's *Shinto*, ya galoot – *Shinto*," Sadie yelled in frustration. "*Shinto*. And don't you knock it."

"Goin' doon on yer knees tae a widdin stick – that's weird," Erchie sneered.

"You treat widdin' goalposts the same wey," Sadie snapped back, "an' besides, they don't get doon on their knees for tae worship sticks. An', don't you forget, they bring much needed work. There's never been any trouble at the factory. Not wan strike. Ye should be thankin' them for a' the work they bring tae this country. The war's been ower a long time, Erchie, it's time tae get on wi' life – and ye need work tae live."

Erchie saw the logic of what Sadie was saying. Many of his drinking pals worked for Japanese and German firms. Some even worked for Indian and Italian firms – delivering curries and pizzas. And, although he hated foreigners he had to admit they sent some crack football players here. Stars who were injecting brilliance into the game. He appreciated the skills of Jorge Alberts and Stefan Klos, both from Germany and playing for the Glasgow Rangers. Erchie had sworn that he would never work for a foreign company not long after he had sworn he'd never work period. But he knew Sadie would nag him until the end of time if he didn't find – or at least make a show of trying to find – employment. He would never ask for his job back at Shakutis. He knew he would never get it anyway. And, besides, he didn't like the look of that wee nyaff or, more to the point, his samurai sword.

"Whit joabs have the Japs brought here wi' the exception o' that Tenko factory Ah used for to be employed in?" he moaned.

"Well, there's Silicon Valley that Ah mentioned before," Sadie said.

"Ah'm no' talkin' aboot breast implants," Erchie said.

"It's got nuthin' tae dae wi' breast implants, Ah telt ye that. It's aboot micro chips an' computers an' things ye don't understaun'."

"Naw, it's you that disnae understaun' Sadie," Erchie snapped back. "Want tae know the reason there's nae trouble at Shakuti's? Well, Ah'll tell ye." Erchie could feel the steam's pressure building up inside his head.

"You tell me then," Sadie said.

"Wan hint o' trouble and youse are frogmarched oot intae the yerd and made for tae dig a hole." Erchie said with a shudder. "Then youse had tae step intae the hole and youse were buried wi' only yer heid stickin' up oot the grun' like a row o' cabbages."

"Ach, ye're bletherin'," Sadie cried, not knowing whether to laugh or weep at Erchie's preposterous statement.

"Youse were there a' day rain, sleet or shine. If ye don't believe me look whit happened tae Big Jimmy McPherson. Five 'oors stuck in the grun', he was, jist his wee heid sticking oot. He was in the Royal Infirmary for five days efter that, the sowel."

"Whit was wrang wi' him?" Sadie asked, knitting her brow, "Hypothermia?"

Erchie shook his head. "Greenfly," he said, stoney-faced.

"Ah've never heard such rubbish in ma life," Sadie said.

"Rubbish is it?" Erchie cried. "Listen. Jimmy's face was beetroot red. His heid had turned a blue colour – a' right if ye're a Rangers supporter, but Jimmy didnae bother wi' fitba' – he supported Partick Thistle. Anywey he was a' embarrassed when he had tae go inte the chemist and ask for somethin' for his rid face and a hairspray."

"Clairol?" Sadie enquired.

"Weed-All," Erchie said.

"Aw, Erchie, yer away wi' the fairies," Sadie said with a slight smile.

"Some o' the blokes suffered frae worms as well," Erchie said.

"Loats of folk hiv worms," Sadie said.

"No' in their heid they don't," Erchie replied. "Ah'm tellin' ye, Sadie, ye couldnae even make a complaint. Fat Hector, oor undercover shop steward, went wan day for to see the wee nyaff aboot a complaint that had been by some o' the wimmen aboot the lavatory doors."

"Whit was wrang wi' the lavatory doors?" Sadie asked with genuine interest.

"They waanted them," Erchie said. "But that's no' the point. Hector was never seen again. His wife eventually got a postcard frae Tokyo sayin' he was trainin' for tae be a pilot wi' Kamikaze Airlines – a subsidiary of Shakuti. His wife was a' excited and thought she would get cheap hoalidays. But that's the last we heard o' him. There's noo a plaque nailed up above his bench."

"Whit does it say?" Sadie asked.

Erchie cleared his throat. "It says – *Big Hector went tae make a complaint. And seein' him again we aint.*"

"You ur paranoid Erchie," Sadie snapped.

"Ah have never suffered frae them in ma life," Erchie said "Ah'm jist angry. Y'know, every mornin' before we was marched through the factory doors, we had a' tae line up facin' the sun and bow oor heids. Ye could be staunin' there for 'oors jist waitin' for the bloody sun tae come oot. Then we had a' tae sing a chorus of *We a' likey worky here.*" Erchie grimaced.

Sadie was beginning to worry about Erchie. She felt he really *was* becoming paranoid. But she could believe half the things he was telling her. He had never shown racist tendencies like he was doing now. She knew, too, that it was not deep rooted. Erchie had always been a very tolerant man. She was surprised once when she walked into their bedroom and saw a large picture of Robert Mugabe, President of Zimbabwe, on the wall. When challenged Erchie said he was a fan. After more questioning, he blushed and admitted he thought it was Al Jolson. But this sudden venom had surprised her although she was sure it was watered down venom.

"Ah do nut believe wan thing you've said, Erchie," she said, standing erect with arms folded defiantly.

"Well, please yersel'," Erchie said with a hurt expression. "But take the case o' Skelly Maisie Kelly. Noo, it's no secret that Maisie likes a wee hauf. Drink was taboo in the workplace and Skelly Maisie was stunned when the wee Nyaff summond her tae his oaffice. 'You like saké?' Well, Maisie isnae wan for tae pass up a drink and was delighted for tae be oaffered a nip frae their national drink."

"So, she got a drink o' saké?" Sadie said, surprised at the wee Nyaff's sudden kind hospitality,

"Naw, the Nyaff used the word 'saké' in the Glesca sense. She got fired."

"Tough!" Sadie exclaimed.

"Ma wee pal, Tyrone, went efter Maisie's joab but got knocked back," Erchie said.

"Nae wonder," Sadie said, "Tyrone is the name o' an Adonis. Wee Tyrone McLatchie is mair like adenoids. Ah suppose he was called efter the beautiful Tyrone Power . . . pity!"

Sadie always thought the name should mirror the image. Tyrone Power was her idol of the silver screen and she felt that Wee Tyrone McLatchie's mother should have been charged under the Trades Description Act. Not only was Tyrone McLatchie diminutive, he was dim, period. Maisie's job at Shakutis would have been ideal. It would have meant constant work with a regular pay poke. Tyrone could only find seasonal employment – usually hiring himself out every spring as a gnome at the B&Q Garden centre or a pixie at Santa's grotto. Shakutis didn't want him as minium height required was five feet. Tyrone lost by half-an-inch. But he was Erchie's china – his pal and Erchie admired how he looked after his ailing old father. They lived alone across the landing from Erchie and Sadie. His mother had run away with a "Shullin-A-Week" man years before. Erchie was angry at Sadie's snide remarks about Tyrone's name.

"He was *nut* called efter Tyrone Power," he said sternly.

"Ah know," Sadie said, "Ah jist said that for to soften the blow of how he really was called Tyrone."

"Tell me," Erchie said with a sigh.

"Well, his faither was there at his birth," Sadie began, "and the minute he saw him poppin' oot he pointed tae a cord lyin' in a coarner an' said, 'Ty-rone rope roon his neck' – get it, 'Tie- rone' – Tyrone. An' that became his name. It was an accident – just like he was."

"Aye, well Ah'll bet his auld faither is gled noo that naebody tied a rope roon' his wean's neck. He'd be loast withoot Wee Ty noo. He's got him runnin' aboot daft efter him – while he lies in bed a' day cuttin' up newspapers." Erchie did not look on Mr McLatchie senior in a good light.

A loud knock at the door startled them for a moment.

"Wonder who that could be?" Erchie said, putting his paper aside and rising. Sadie stopped him.

"Ah'll get it," she said. Opening the door Tyrone McLatchie swept in. "Hi, Sadie – Erchie," he gushed.

"Oh, it's yersel', Ty," Sadie greeted him with a grimace.

"How's it gone, china?" Erchie smiled.

"Ah jist came in fur tae see if ye're finished wi' yer paper?" Ty blurted out.

"Can ye no' buy yer ain paper?" Sadie said, annoyed.

"Ah bought the *Daily Record* last week and went frae page wan tae the last page and couldnae understaun' wan word."

"How no'?" Sadie asked.

"Ah canny read," Tyrone said.

"So, whit dae ye want the paper for, then?" Sadie said, puzzled.

"It's for ma Da'," Ty said.

"Can he read, then?" Erchie piped up

"Oh, aye, he can read . . . but that's no' whit he wants the paper for," Ty said.

"Well, Ah'm no' supplyin' yer faither's toilet requirements," Sadie snapped. "We ur always the wan replenishin' the supply doon there. It's aboot time somebody else took a turn – Auld Cecil Boag, for instance, he gets the *London Times* – there's enough there for tae last a month."

"Naw, ye don't understaun'. He uses it for his origami," Ty said by way of an explanation.

"His *whit?*" Sadie cried.

"His *origami*," Tyrone explained.

"Another bloody Japanese import," Erchie sneered. "They're up tae everythin'. Ye canny trust them. Ye'll soon be gettin'

Sukiyaki instead o' porridge for yer breakfast." Erchie spat out the words.

"That's a funny name – Sukiyaki," Sadie said.

"Only folk wi' nae teeth wull appreciate it," Erchie said, "That's who the Japs invented it for – *sooky* – get it?"

"An' whit aboot *yaki*?" Tyrone asked, thinking of his gumsy father.

"Yaki – means talk – yakity-yak – get it? It means ye can talk wi' yer teeth oot – *sooky-yaki*. For first thing in the moarnin' it's a perfect breakfast – dead clever they wee men."

"Never mind that," Sadie said. "Here, gie him that and see whit he makes o' it." Erchie handed over his paper.

"Oh, he'll put it tae good use," Tyrone said proudly. "He shapes things and he cuts up the paper as well and turns it intae paper sculptures, so he does." Tyrone's chest inflated three inches. "He is very artistic ma Da'," he went on. "Ye know he wance made a full-size model o' Mrs Thatcher – he's very fond o' Mrs Thatcher."

The name of the former Prime Minister made Erchie grimace. "He's no' only artistic, he's daft as well," he said sarcastically.

"His Mrs Thatcher is a dead, spittin' image," Ty twittered. "Ye want tae see it?"

"Ye've still got it?" Sadie asked.

"Oh, aye, he widnae part wi' it. It lies at the fit o' his bed," Ty said.

"Away an' get it," Erchie said.

Tyrone was out the door in a flash.

"But don't bring yer faither in," Sadie called after him.

Tyrone was obviously very proud of his father's artistic prowess with nothing more than some old newspapers, a pair of scissors and his arthritic hands. He wondered why he hadn't picked up the same genes. All he could draw was his broo money. His father should be recognised by the nation. He should be exhibited in the Kelvingrove Art Galleries. Many others also agreed he should be hung.

Turning to Erchie, Sadie snapped," Whit dae you want tae see Mrs Thatcher for?"

"Ah dae hiv ma ain masochistic moments," he said quietly.

"Aye, right enough," Sadie said, "It's only right that you should

22

dae some penance noo an' again."

Tyrone was back in no time. Standing in the middle of the room, he held up the full-size paper sculpture of Mrs Thatcher. Whilst the body was comprised of newsprint, a large coloured photo of her face was stuck on a large, smiling head. Holding it by the shoulders he said proudly, "There – whit dae ye think?"

Erchie stood up, walked across the room and, hands on hips, stood and surveyed old McLatchie's masterpiece.

"Mmm – no' bad!" he said. "Aye, no' bad at a'."

Sadie made no comment.

"He wanted for tae make Pavarotti but he didnae hiv enough paper," Tyrone said.

"Ah suppose it *is* creative," Erchie said at last.

"Creative?" Sadie cried, "An' whit dae *you* know aboot creative?"

"Mair than you, that's for sure," Erchie retorted.

"Listen tae the art critic for the *Observer*. Whit aboot the time you, me an' Bunty went tae the Kelvingrove Art Galleries and you were showin' aff yer knowledge of fine art – tryin' tae impress everybody. Ye thought *Whistler's Mother* was Ronnie Ronalde's maw."

"That was a genuine mistake. If that's a' ye've got on me ye've got nothin'." Erchie was pleased with himself.

"That's no' a'," Sadie said. "Ye really gave me a red face when in front o' a crowd o' people ye cried ower the attendant an' asked who the brilliant artist was that created that sculpture made wi' green-painted bricks on a vertical shape. An' he said it was the Gent's toilet."

"Ma Da's disappointed that Ah'm no' mair artistic," Tyrone said sadly, " He says Ah should start workin' in cley."

"Frae six feet doon?" Sadie said facetiously.

"Ah must admit Ah'm a bit creative masel'," Erchie said pompously.

"In that case Ah suggest ye get doon tae Shakutis and create a joab for yersel'," Sadie sniped. "Get doon on yer knees and grovel if ye hiv tae."

"*Grovel*? *Me* grovel?" Erchie yelled. "Ah hiv never grovelled in ma life – except for the time when Ah got doon on ma knees in front o' yer faither – pleadin'. "

23

"Wur ye pleadin' for Sadie's haun' in marriage?" Tyrone sighed.

"Naw, he had a shotgun in his haun' and was demandin' Ah take every bit o' her."

"So, whit wur ye pleadin' for?" Tyrone asked, puzzled.

"Ah was pleadin' wi' him tae pull the trigger," Erchie said, not glancing at Sadie.

Tyrone glanced sadly at Sadie.

"Y'see, Tyrone," Sadie said, "ma Da' was a very religious man and wanted tae make an honest wumman o' me – know whit Ah mean?"

Tyrone nodded. He understood. "He wanted ye tae become a nun?" he said.

"Naw, naw, nothin' like that," Sadie snapped. "He just wanted tae make an honest wumman o' me – see?"

"Wur ye a shoplifter?" Tyrone looked worried.

"Naw, naw," she said, then, standing straight and clearing her throat, she said loudly. "Ah was expectin' oor Bunty."

"Where was she?" Tyrone asked.

"She was at Barraland, where the hell dae ye think she was?" Erchie bawled.

"That was nae reason for him gonny shoot you, then, was it?" Tyrone said sternly.

"Jist forget it, Tyrone," Sadie capitulated.

"There was only wan thing wrang. Her faither, bein' the religious man he was, wanted the wean tae have a saint's name. There's nae Saint Bunty and he wanted the wean for tae be called Roger."

"There's nae Saint Roger either as faur as Ah know," Tyrone volunteered. "Besides Bunty's a lassie and there's nae lassies called Roger – except maybe Ginger."

"He was hopin' for a boy wean. Anywey, ma maw was a very holy wumman tae. She was gled the wean wisnae called Roger. She wanted for tae call Bunty Maria Louisa San Salvador Jacinta Rodriguez Barcelona Bridie Hunter – efter her granny."

"Was her granny Welsh?" Tyrone asked.

"German," Sadie said.

"Ah knew it, Ah knew it," Erchie cried. "Ah should've known you had German blood in ye that first day Ah met yer maw."

24

Erchie was fuming.

"Whit aboot ma maw?" Sadie said, narrowing her eyes.

"She wore a cross roon her neck," Erchie said.

"Ah telt ye she was a very holy wumman, didn't Ah? Loats of holy wimmen wear crosses roon their neck."

"No' the Iron Cross First Class, they don't," Erchie snapped.

"Ach, shut yer face," Sadie said. "Ye're just an auld saurkraut."

Erchie exploded. "Look at that," he bellowed. "She canny even say cabbage. A'right, *mein frau*," he said clicking his heels and giving a Nazi salute. "May your Beirwurst be the worst beer you've ever tasted."

"Ma maw was a wee holy wumman tae," Tyrone volunteered. "She used tae light caunle's a' ower the hoose."

"That's nice," Sadie said. "Was it tae say her prayers?"

"Naw. oor electricity was always cut aff," Tyrone said innocently.

"Naebody was mair holy than her maw," Erchie stepped in. "She had statues o' saints a' ower the hoose."

"A loat o' devout people had statues o' saints in the hoose," Sadie snapped.

"No' six feet concrete wans they don't," Erchie rasped.

Tyrone was taking all this in. "Lookin' at you two," he said, "Ah don't think Ah'll ever get married."

"Naebody would hiv ye," Erchie said, unkindly.

Tyrone looked hurt..

"Don't you believe it," Sadie said. comforting him, "there's plenty o' lassies would gie their eye teeth tae be goin oot wi' you."

Tyrone felt better. "Ah know," he said, "Every lassie Ah've been oot wi' has did just that."

"Whit dae ye mean?" Sadie asked.

"They've a' been gumsy. Ah didnae mind 'cos it saved me buyin' them carmels."

"Teeth disnae matter, Tyrone," Sadie said. Then, pointing to her chest, she added, "It's whit ye've got in here, Tyrone. That's whit counts."

"Ma wallet?" Tyrone said, his hand coming up to his chest.

"Yer hert, Tyrone, yer hert. Look at Bella McGinty – she had the nicest smile in the street."

"Only at weekends, Sadie," Erchie interrupted.

"Even wi' her beautiful teeth she couldnae get a boyfriend," Sadie added.

"How no'?" Tyrone asked.

"Halitosis," Sadie said.

"Whit's that?" Tyrone asked, drawing down his brows.

"Bad breath," Sadie said. "Her boyfriends couldnae look her straight in the eye."

"How no'?"

"They were a' wearin' gas masks. But she didnae hiv it here either," Sadie pointed to her chest. "She treated her boyfriends like dirt. Everybody started callin' her Dyson. So, ye see, her smile didn't count. So the next time ye go oot wi' a gumsy lassie – be thankful."

"Just gie her a plate o' Sukiyaki, Ty," Erchie laughed.

Tyrone would never consider marriage. Not while his old man lay in that bed. The old man was devastated when his wife ran off with the "Shullin'-A-Week" man. The old man missed him. They used to play chess when he called every week to collect for his clothing cheque company. The games stopped when one Friday night the wee man failed to turn up and his fat wife vanished. The old man put away the chess set and went to bed and had been there ever since. For weeks he just lay staring at the ceiling and Tyrone was beside himself with worry. He had tried everything to bring his father out of his semi-comatose position. He had installed a television set at the foot of the bed hoping he would capture his father's interest. It was seeing a programme on Origami that caught the old boy's attention and Tyrone was delighted. He felt his father was taking an unhealthy interest in Tinky-Winky of Teletubbies fame.

"Ah'll never get married while ma da' needs me," he said with a sigh. "He jist lies there and stares and stares a' the time wishin' he was back where he was born." A lump came to Tyrone's throat.

Sadie, too, felt a lump coming to her throat.

"Where was that, Tyrone?" she asked.

"The Planet o' the Apes?" Erchie cried facetiously.

"China," Tyrone said.

Erchie and Sadie cried out together, "*China?*"

Tyrone nodded. "Aye, he was born in a Paddy Field," he said proudly.

"Ach, in that case he's no' a Chinaman," Erchie said, "he's an Irishman."

But Tyrone was adamant. "Naw, naw," he said, "he was born in Paddy Field in China," he argued.

"If your faither was born in a Paddy field then Ah'm a Chinaman," Erchie scoffed.

"Ah can prove it tae ye," Tyrone said, pulling out a piece of paper in triumph. "This," he said brandishing the document with a flourish, "is his birth certificate. Ah had tae get it oot tae find his right date o' birth for the society man. It's auld an' the writin's no' very clear but look, there ye are, "Born in a Paddy – errr it's a wee bit blurred – field."

"Let me see that," Erchie snapped, grabbing the paper. "Sadie, get me that magnifyin' gless frae the sideboard," he commanded.

Sadie shrugged and produced the glass. Erchie surveyed the paper closely until finally he threw up his arms in triumph.

"Ya eejit!" he cried, "Paddy field – *look*." He thrust the paper under Tyrone's nose and jabbed the paper with his finger. "*Look*," he cried. "In Paddy's *Market*. Yer faither was born in Glesca – in *Paddy's Market*."

Tyrone was stunned. He always thought his father was a Chinaman but to be born in Paddy's Market, Glasgow's famous street market, was a big disappointment.

Seeing his disappointment, Sadie put a comforting arm around his shoulder. "Never mind, son," she said softly, "ye can always get a take-away chow mein if ye feel nostalgic."

Erchie drew Sadie a look and ruffled his paper. "Ah'll gie ye this paper in a minute for yer auld man – although the auld swine disnae deserve it," he said gruffly.

"That's no' nice," Tyrone retorted. "Ma da' is a good, decent man, so he is."

"Decent?" Erchie snapped. "He hadnae the decency for tae be born a Chinaman, did he? He should've known you'd be disappointed."

"*You* ur the biggest disappointment in the present company," Sadie said angrily. "Ye jist canny keep a joab, can ye?"

"Ah canny help it if ma talents ur never recognised," Erchie said grumpily.

"It's yer face that's recognised," Sadie said. "You've got Foot an' Mooth disease. Ye open yer mooth an' put yer foot in it. Ye're an ignorant get."

"Ah am nut ignorant," Erchie said, hurt.

"Erchie, you think the Weakest Link is a skinny sausage," Sadie sniped. "Ye've a knack o' gettin' sacked – ye're a professional. Ye're assured o' yer Broo money if ye're sacked. Ye know a' the dodges – how tae get fired in wan easy lesson. Ye're known as the Giro Kid. And on top o' a' that you're a racist. Tyrone, jist as well ye're no' a Chinaman or ye widnae be staunin' here right now."

Tyrone grimaced.

"That's a lie," Erchie said sharply, "When Ah first met Tyrone Ah thought he was frae Siberia."

"Whit made ye think that?" Sadie asked drawing down her brows.

"He spoke in a high pitched voice," Erchie said.

"Know whit your daein', Erchie?" Sadie snapped.

"Naw, whit am Ah daein'?" Erchie said.

"You are jist talkin' a loat o' waffle for tae take ma mind aff your stupidity," Sadie said angrily.

"Whit dae ye mean?" Erchie snapped.

"Ye loast yer joab – fired. Ye're always gettin' fired."

"It wisnae ma fault," Erchie said, sulking. "It never is," Sadie said.

Erchie sighed. He knew Sadie was right. He just could not keep a job. But that was only because he was always employed, in his way of thinking, in menial tasks. The world owed him better things. He had been cut out for higher things. Even his teacher at school had recognised his talent. Didn't he once say, "Erchie, you ur gonny go down in history." Erchie was delighted. The fact that he also went down in geography, maths and English didn't count.

"Shakutis are no' gonny get away wi' firin' me," Erchie said with a grunt. "Ah wull get ma own back on them, so Ah wull." He took up his paper, gave it a ruffle and began to read.

Tyrone looked questioningly at Sadie. "He's gonny dae whit General Macarthur did, Tyrone," Sadie said with sarcasm. "He's gonny take on the Japs. Don't you forget, Erchie," she went on pointing at her husband with a shaking finger, "Macarthur said 'I shall return' – so that's whit *you* better be plannin'.""

"Huh!" Erchie said, ruffling his paper vigorously.

"Aw, Ah hate for tae see ye like this, Erchie," Tyrone said sadly.

"Don't you worry aboot him, Tyrone," Sadie said. "Ah'll dae a' the worryin'. You've got enough tae worry ye, so ye hiv." Sadie had genuine concern in her voice.

It was enough to make Erchie look up. "Whit's *he* got tae worry aboot," he snapped. "He hisnae loast his joab. He's never had wan."

"He's got his auld faither tae worry aboot," Sadie sniped.

"Whit's he got tae worry aboot him for?" Erchie replied. "He lies in his bed a' day playin' wi' his origami. Whit's tae worry aboot that?"

"Tyrone grew up thinkin' his faither was a Chinaman and that his ancestors were emperors an' that. But tae suddenly be telt ye ur nut decended frae a great Chinese dynasty but yer faither was born in Paddy's Market."

"Aye, that was a terrible blow," Tyrone said.

"There's nuthin' wrang wi' bein' born in Paddy's Market," Erchie said. "Look at Bowely Broon – he was born in a pub."

"How did that happen?" Tyrone asked.

"Well," Erchie began, "his maw an' da' was oot for a walk wan day an' his maw was expectin' at the time – although she didnae know it was Wee Bowely, if ye know whit Ah mean. Anywey, his da' got thirsty and they nipped intae a pub for a nip and came oot wi' a nipper – see?"

"Aw, that's romantic!" Tyrone smiled.

"Aye, he goes back tae his roots every chance he gets," Sadie said sarcastically, referring to Erchie's constantly inebriated pal.

"Aye, well aw ma life Ah thought Ah was born in tae a great dynasty – an' Ah'm no'," Tyrone said.

"An' whit dynasty was that, Tyrone?" Sadie asked, showing interest.

"Ming," Tyrone said.

"Ach, well," Erchie cried, "ye're lucky ye're no'. Who would want for tae be associated wi' the Ming crowd?"

"Ach, away – ye don't know whit ye're talkin' aboot," Sadie snapped.

"Aye Ah dae," Erchie protested.

"Whit dae you know aboot Chinese history?" Sadie retorted. "Whit dae you know aboot the great Emperor Ming?"

"He was the baddie in Flash Gordon," Erchie said, triumph in his voice.

"Ya ignorant get!" Sadie cried, "The baddie in Flash Gordon," she mocked. "Ming was the maker of top quality vases," she added, knowingly.

"The thing is, Tyrone," Erchie said, "ye wurnae born a China man. Ming has got nothin' tae dae wi' you or yer faither. In fact nane o' the two o' youse have probably never known an oriental."

"Ah know wan," Tyrone said smugly.

"Who?" Erchie said in disbelief.

"Wee Maggie Paterson," Tyrone said.

"*Wee Maggie Paterson?*" Sadie and Erchie cried in unison.

Tyrone nodded. "Aye, she was a stoater," Tyrone said.

"She disnae sound Oriental," Sadie said.

"Sounds mair Brigton," Erchie volunteered.

"Naw, she was definitely Indian," Tyrone said. "She was born in the Taj Mahal."

"In India?" Erchie said, raising his eyebrows.

"Naw, in Govan Road," Tyrone said. "Her maw went there for tae buy a curry when she felt somethin' stirrin' in her stomach."

"Aye, some curries dae hiv that affect oan ye," Sadie said with conviction.

"Before her maw knew whit was happenin' there was wee Maggie bawlin' her heid aff right in the middle o' her vindaloo." Tyrone said, pleased with himself.

"Her maw should' ve called her Nan," Sadie said.

"Efter her granny?" Tyrone asked, puzzled.

"Naw, efter the breid that goes wi' the vindaloo," Sadie laughed.

"Well, anywey," Tyrone went on, "efter that, Wee Maggie thought of hersel' as bein' Indian, so she did."

Erchie shook his head vigorously.

"Naw, naw," he cried, "it disnae work that wey. There is certain pprer . . . er . . . preog . . . er . . . rules regardin' that. For instance if your maw was travellin' oan an American plane or was visitin' an American Embassy and you was born then you would be an American citizen. Because you're born in an Indian restaurant disnae make you an Indian. Restaurants don't count, Ty. If that was the case a helluva loat o' us would be foreigners."

"How dae ye make that oot?" Tyrone asked, drawing his brows together.

"It's just the wey things ur," Erchie said. "Ah mean if we go by that pre . . . er . . . pregnosis, Ah should be an Italian."

"How come?" Tyrone asked.

"Ah was born in Valente's chip shoap in London Road. Ma maw went in tae buy a fish supper and it was me she got," Erchie said.

"Well, justice was done there," Sadie said. "She came oot the shoap wi' a haddy."

Erchie ignored Sadie's sarcasm.

"Ur ye sure it wisnae a puddin' she asked for?" Sadie added, turning the screw.

"Ah wull treat that comment wi' the contempt it deserves," Erchie said. "But ye see whit Ah mean, Ty, don't ye?"

"Naw," Tyrone said, shaking his head.

Erchie threw up his hands in despair.

" Ah believe that you ur whit you ur. It's whit's in yer blood," Tyrone said with authority. " Yer genes is the thing. Ye ur whit yer genes say ye ur. It's yer blood that counts. Ye ur whit yer blood says ye ur, so ye ur." Tyrone was pleased with himself.

"Naw, naw, "Erchie argued, "That's no' true. Whit if ye hiv a blood transfusion? Ah mean ye don't know who's blood ye've got in yer veins. Wance, when Ah was oan hoaliday in Majorca, Ah got knoacked doon and had for tae hiv a blood transfusion. Noo, Ah could hiv any kind o' blood in me. If it's frae a local that disnae make me a Spaniard."

"Ah see yer point," Tyrone said. "Cos if it was frae a dug that disnae mean y're a dug."

"Ye're catchin' on, Tyrone," Erchie said." Noo, when ma maw was expectin' me she went intae Goldberg's for tae buy her weddin' dress an' Ah was born in wimmen's underwear – noo, whit dae ye think that makes me,eh?"

"A transvestite?" Tyrone asked innocently.

"Don't be so bloody stupid," Erchie cried, a naughty twinkle in his eye. "It jist makes me premature. It disnae mean because Ah was born in Goldbergs that Ah'm a Jew. Jist like if Ah had been born in the Vatican it widnae mean that Ah'm the Pope."

"Ur ye?" Tyrone asked.

"Am Ah Jewish?" Erchie replied.

"Naw, ur ye the Pope." Tyrone was serious.

"Don't be so daft," Erchie cried.

"Tyrone," Sadie said. "He's as near as dammit. There's nuthin' he'd like better than for tae sit on that chair a' day and hiv me cairryin' him aboot in it."

"Aw, very funny," Erchie said screwing up his lips. "A' Ah'm trying for to say is that Tyrone disnae know whit he's talkin' aboot."

"Well, if your pregnant maw went intae Goldbergs for to buy her weddin' dress nut only does that no' make you Jewish but we a' know fine well whit it *does* make ye, don't we?" Sadie sniped.

"Ye mean Erchie's a . . . a . . ?" Tyrone stammered

"Aye, and a lazy wan at that," Sadie replied.

"There's she goes again. Ye know it wisnae ma fault that ma services wur no longer required at Shakutis for reasons known only tae that wee Jap Nyaff," Erchie said huffily.

"Aye, well, wee Nyaff or no'," Sadie said, "you get yer joab back or nut only wull ye be cairried aboot in a chair ye'll be cairried aboot in a stretcher."

"Aye," Tyrone said, "it's no good for a man no' tae work. It is bad for his molar."

"Moral, Tyrone," Sadie corrected, "although his molars might just come intae it when Ah punch his teeth oot."

Erchie turned on Tyrone. "Whit dae *you* know aboot work," Erchie snapped. "You've never worked in yer life."

Tyrone shuffled his feet. "There's a very good reason for that," he mumbled. "It's ma heart."

"Whit's yer heart got ta dae wi' you no' workin'?" Erchie asked, puzzled.

"It's no' in it," Tyrone replied, not batting an eyelid.

Erchie glanced at Sadie and shook his head, a look of despair on his face. He took up his newspaper, gave it one quick ruffle and began to read.

Tyrone said nothing. His mind was racing fast. He felt that his Paddy Market father had conned him. All his life he looked on himself as Chinese. How could his old dad take him in like this?

Why had the old man a habit of calling him Wee Pooh when he was a schoolboy? And Dung when he grew up? Sadie left the room, giving Erchie a contemptuous look. Erchie ignored her.

"Wimmin!" he grimaced. "An' get *her* oot o' here," he snapped, pointing a shaking finger at the cut-out of Margaret Thatcher.

Tyrone carefully placed the former Prime Minister on a chair, making sure she was comfortable.

"Ah don't want for tae go in and disturb ma da' the noo. So, if ye don't mind Ah'll place her here."

Erchie grunted. "Plug her in," he said.

"Is it wan o' they chairs that goes up an' doon the stairs itsel'," he asked, looking desperately around the room for a staircase.

"Don't be stupit!" Erchie said, "Ah was talkin' aboot – och, never mind," he said waving a contemptuous hand.

"Ah'll put her in the cupboard the noo if she gies ye the hee-bie-jeebies," Tyrone said, putting the cut-out away.

"Boy, ur the mice in there in for shock," Erchie laughed. "That's nae disrespect tae yer faither, Tyrone," he added. "But Ah'd prefer that she was put oot the road before oor Bunty brings up her new boyfriend. Ah mean, he could be of a different political persuasion. He might even be non-commital. Personally Ah feel a' politicians should definitely be committed."

Sadie entered the room, duster in hand. She went straight to the cupboard to fetch her feather duster. Opening the door, she let out a yell.

"Oh my God!" she gasped, holding her hand to her heart. "Whit a fright Ah got there. Ah opened that door and saw Mrs Thatcher starin' at me."

"We jist put her in there in case Bunty's boyfriend took offence," Erchie said without looking up from his paper.

"Aye, well ye can jist get her oot o' there," Sadie snapped," Ah don't want for to be frightened every time Ah go intae the cupboard."

Erchie nodded to Tyrone who got the message. The wee man retrieved his father's art work from the cupboard and propped it on a chair by the table.

"Whit were ye sayin' aboot Bunty's boyfriend?" Sadie asked.

Erchie shrugged. "We don't know anythin' aboot him, dae we?

Ah mean, we've never seen him. Usually she brings up her new boyfriends right away. Dae ye think there's somethin' wrang wi' this wan?"

"Maybe he's frightened for tae meet you," Tyrone said.

"Ye may well be right, Tyrone," Sadie said.

"Whit dae ye mean by that?" Erchie said, hurt.

"Ye terrorise Bunty's boyfriends, so ye dae," Sadie said. "Mind that nice boy she brought up an efter he left this hoose he went away for to become a priest?"

"So, whit's wrang wi' that?" Erchie said, "Ah didnae fancy him. It must've been in him frae the start for tae become a priest. Ah saved oor Bunty frae terrible heartbreak, so Ah did." Erchie was pleased with himself.

Tyrone agreed. He nodded his approval. "Aye, ye're right, Erchie," he said. "He must've been gonny be a priest right frae the start."

"Erchie," Sadie cried, " he was a grand master in the Orange Ludge."

Once again Erchie shrugged. "People can turn," Erchie said.

"Hiv you ever turned, Erchie?" Tyrone asked.

Erchie nodded. "Ah hiv turned many a time . . . the last time bein' last Friday," Erchie said.

"Ye never telt me," Tyrone said. "Whit happened?"

"Ah was walkin' doon Gallygate," Erchie said, "when Ah suddenly turned intae a pub."

Erchie chuckled and Tyrone laughed loudly.

"Aw, ye had me goin' there," Tyrone said.

"It's aboot time ye wur," Sadie said.

Tyrone ignored Sadie's comment. "Whit does Bunty's boyfriend dae, Sadie?" he asked.

"He's a horticulturist," Sadie said, pride in her voice.

"That's marvellous so it is," Tyrone said in admiration. "Imagine that. It would be great for to hiv wan o' them in the family," he clicked his teeth.

"Ah am nut a bit interested," Erchie said ruffling his paper. "We need wan o' them like we need a hole in the heid."

"Ye never know, Erchie," Tyrone sad. "Er . . . whit is it anywey?"

"Ah've nae idea," Erchie said.

"That's because you're an ignorant, racist get," Sadie snapped.

"Well then, smart-ass, you tell us whit is a hort . . . a horror . . . wan o' them things?" Erchie asked grimly.

"He's intae gardenin' – flooers an' plants an' that. He specialises in Bonsai Trees."

"Ah knew it. Ah knew it," Erchie exploded. "Ah knew there was a reason Bunty hidnae brought hom up. He's a Jap, int he?" Steam jetted from Erchie's ears.

"Ah don't know if he's Japanese or no' and Ah don't care if he's frae Mars," Sadie said angrily.

"Whit's Bonsai Trees?" Tyrone asked naively.

"They ur Japanese trees, Tyrone," Erchie explained, "an' they're jist aboot twelve inches tall."

"They sound quite nice," Tyrone said smiling.

"No' if yer dug's a Great Dane, Tyrone. Ah'm tellin' ye they ur miniaturisin' everythin'. That wee Nyaff came intae the factory wan day wi' a wee animal the size o' a moose oan a lead. Ah asked him whit it was and know whit he said?"

Tyrone shook his head.

"He said it was a hoarse," Erchie was contemptuous.

Sadie was listening intently to this conversation and sadly shook her head. She knew Erchie had a vivid imagination but felt he was painting Shakutis bad for her benefit. She knew that Erchie not only didn't want to work there but didn't want to work period. He had already made up his mind that Bunty's boyfriend was Japanese. She felt she could keep quiet no longer.

"Listen pieface," she snapped, "You ur talkin' a loat o' rubbish. You are fillin' Tyrone's heid wi' garbage as if there's no' enough in there already. Shakutis and firms like them have brought much needed joabs tae this country. And probably every wan o' them have their 'Wee Nyaffs'. But so dae many Scoattish firms. Gie somebody a brass button and they become dictators. It disnae matter whit colour their skin is or where in this world they come frae. You ur an ignorant racist. Ah don't care whit Bunty's boyfreen's race is. He's no' Japanese that's for sure. The boy's name is Herman and ye don't get a Japanese boy wi' a name like that." Sadie was puffing with anger.

Tyrone agreed with her. "Sadie's right, Erchie," he said, "Herman's no' a Jap name. He's probably Welsh."

But Erchie was fuming. "Away ye go ya wee idiot," he said throwing daggers at his crony. "*Herman*?" he bellowed, "Herman the *German*. That's jist as bad. "

"You ur livin' in the past, Erchie," Sadie said. "Admit it. You've got it in for Shakutis no' because they're Japanese. It's because they sacked you. Ye'll jist no' admit it."

"That is nut true," Erchie said, avoiding Sadie's eyes.

Tyrone took his courage in his hands. Coughing nervously, he said, "Sadie could be right, Erchie, You've always made it plain ye didnae like oor wee Japanese freen's. Ah first suspected it when ma lovely wee hoose-trained dug wandered intae your hoose an' Ah never saw it again."

"Whit's that got tae dae wi' the Japs?" Erchie snapped. "Was it a Shihtzu dug?"

"Naw, Ah telt ye it was hoose trained," Tyrone said in his dog's defence.

"It was a Jap dug, wint it?" Erchie almost spat the words.

"Chinese," Tyrone said.

"Same as yer faither nearly was?" Erchie said sarcastically." Ah had nothin' tae dae wi' yer dug's disappearance. Maybe it ran oot intae the street and was caught and turned intae a curry."

"Aw, ye don't think that, Erchie, dae ye?" Tyrone said, distressed.

"Ye can never tell, Tyrone," Erchie said, "Many curries Ah've ate tasted like shihtzu."

"Maybe that's why ye talk a loat o that," Sadie said.

"Don't be so vulgar," Erchie said. "You ur just tryin' for tae wind me up so that Ah'll go an' beg for ma joab back. Even sayin' that Bunty's boyfriend's called Herman. That's no' true, int it no'?"

Sadie had a whimsical smile on her face. She *was* getting to her husband and she was enjoying his squirming.

"Int it no'?" Erchie repeated. "Tell me his name's no' Herman."

"Aw right, Erchie, Ah was jist kiddin' ye on," Sadie said. "Ah knew that would aggravate ye."

Erchie sighed with great relief. "Thank God for that!" he said, "Don't ever frighten me like that again, Sadie. Ye nearly gave me a heart attack. Whit is his name anywey?"

"Adolph," Sadie said with a straight face.

Erchie threw up his arms. "*Adolph . . . Adolph?*" he hollered. "Geez, that's worse."

"Ah think it's a nice Irish name," Tyrone said.

"*Irish?*" Erchie threw daggers at his pal. "Away ya daft idiot. Adolph is a Teutonic name . . . *Teutonic.* You know whit that is, Tyrone, don't ye?"

Tyrone nodded. "Of course Ah dae. It's a wine: Buckfast Teutonic Wine – everybody knows that." Tyrone was pleased with himself.

"It's got nothin' tae dae wi' a wine, ya wee imbicile. *Teutonic* . . . think aboot it, Tyrone."

Tyrone thought deeply. His eyes a window of deep thinking and puzzlement. Then, snapping his fingers, he lit up.

"Ye're right, Erchie, whit a dimwit Ah am. Tuetonic – how did Ah no' see that. It was a plague that swept the country in the auld days. The Teutonic Plague . . . it was cairried by rats."

Erchie shook his head in despair and Sadie hid a chuckle.

"It's got nothin' tae dae wi' a plague, Tyrone. It's a German name – Adolph. It was Hitler's name."

Tyrone shrugged. "It disnae mean he's a German just because his name's Adolph, so it disnae," he said authoratively. "Ah wance knew a bloke who's name was Declan."

"And whit was he – Mongolian?" Erchie asked.

Tyrone shook his head. "Irish," he said.

Erchie glanced at Sadie and turned his gaze towards heaven.

"Imagine that!" Tyrone said.

"It disnae matter whether Bunty's boyfriend is German, Japanese, Mongolian or anythin' else. He's her choice and he wull be welcome in this hoose, d'ye hear me, Erchie?" It was not a question. It was a command.

Erchie grimaced and said nothing.

"Ah'll get ma own back on that crowd doon at Shakutis if it's the last thing Ah dae," he said through gritted teeth.

"Aye, ye'll get yer own joab back," Sadie snapped.

"Watch ye don't dae anythin' daft, Erchie," Tyrone volunteered, "or ye could end up in court wi' yer name in the papers."

"His name wull be in the papers a'right if he disnae dae whit he's telt," Sadie said angrily. "In the Obituary column."

37

"Ah had ma name in tha papers wance," Tyrone said proudly.

"Aye, Ah remember," Erchie said, "and ye got a red face – a showin' up, so ye did."

"Whit was that a' aboot, Tyrone. Ah don't remember that," Sadie said quizzically.

"It was when you were away visitin' yer maw in Disneyland," Erchie said.

"Ma maw was never in Disneyland," Sadie snapped.

"Aye, well, she should've been," Erchie retorted. Sadie ignored Erchie's facetiousness.

"How did ye get yer name in the paper, Tyrone?" she said.

"It was the time Ah reported seein' Crop Circles," Tyrone said.

"Aye, well, some people think they're caused by aliens." Sadie said. "Ah can see why it would cause an interest and get yer name in the papers. So, how did that gie ye a showin' up,then?"

"Sadie, ye don't get crop circles in Argyle Steet," Erchie said.

Sadie burst out laughing. "That was yer big minute of fame, then, Tyrone, eh?" she chuckled.

" How was Ah tae know they was caused by a wee man shovin' a barra that had loast its left-sided wheel?" Tyrone said. "Aye, an' they had ma photay in as well," Tyrone added. "Ah was plastered a' ower Glesca. Ah bought up a' the papers Ah could get and gave them tae ma da' and that kept him busy for months. Somebody said that we a' hiv fifteen minutes of fame in this world. Ah think it was Andy Cameron."

"Naw, naw," Sadie said, shaking her head. "Ah think it was another Andy – Andy er – Andy . . ." she searched for words.

"Warhol," Erchie volunteered."

"Aye, Ah think it wis him," Sadie said.

Silence once more fell amongst them. Erchie ruffled his paper and continued to read. Tyrone shuffled his feet, Sadie continued to dust and Margaret Thatcher sat comfortably on her chair. Tyrone gave a slight cough.

"Ah – er – wull just get in and see that ma da's a' right, then," he said, "Ye – ye – er – no' finished wi' yer paper, ur ye?"

"In a minute, Ty, in a minute," Erchie said impatiently.

Silence fell once more.

"He could be an Eskimo," Tyrone said breaking the spell.

"Who could?" Erchie said, looking up.

"Your Bunty's boyfreen'," Tyrone said.

"Whit ur ye talkin' aboot?" Sadie said. "Ma Bunty disnae know any Eskimos. There's no' many live aroon' here, Tyrone."

"She could dae worse than mairryin' an Eskimo," Tyrone said.

"She's no' goin' wi' an Eskimo, Tyrone," Erchie snapped, then looking to Sadie added, "Is she?"

"Ah don't know an' Ah don't care," Sadie said, shrugging. "She can go wi' a Martian as faur as Ah'm concerned. Whoever oor Bunty wants is a'right by me. She's a sensible lassie."

"They're very clever people, them Eskimos," Tyrone said. "Ah've seen them on the Telly. Nae supermarkets for them, y'know. They jist go oot, dig a hole in the street and pull oot a fish - nae bother - and sometimes a seal - they're experts." Tyrone was full of admiration.

"Don't be stupit," Erchie said. "Can ye really see oor Bunty's man sayin' he wis goin' oot no' tae the pub like normal men or the bookies or that. But wi' a cheery wave sayin', "Ah'm jist goin' doon tae the street for tae catch a fish - away ye go."

"Well, Bunty says they're goin' oot tae a fancy-dress party this week and he's comin' up for tae pick her up. So we'll soon see whit he is no' that it matters," Sadie emphasised.

"Aw, this sounds serious," Erchie said, screwing up his nose, "he's comin' up here, eh?"

"Whit's the big deal?" Sadie said. "Bunty's had scores o' boyfreens an had them up tae the hoose."

"Aye, well, Ah must admit that oor Bunty can get the boyfreens a'right. She's a good lookin' lassie when she puts her teeth in," Erchie said proudly.

"Ah didnae know your Bunty wore falsies," Tyrone said in genuine surprise.

"Only her teeth, Tyrone," Erchie said quickly, "only her teeth."

"Ye'd never know," Tyrone said.

"Aye and she would never have lost her ain beautiful white teeth if she hadnae been goin' wi' a dental mechanic," Sadie said, some bitterness in her voice.

"Whit dae ye mean?" Tyrone asked, puzzled.

"Well, y'see," Sadie began, "his business was failin' and oor Bunty got a' her teeth oot just for tae put some business his way.

39

"She's awfu' considerate, oor Bunty," Erchie added.

"Aye, she's like that," Sadie said. "A' love and nae teeth."

"He made her a set for nothin'," Erchie said.

" Ah'll bet he was that pleased wi' her devotion an' that," Tyrone said.

"Ah suppose he was," Sadie said. "He liked nothin' better than for tae see her sittin' there smilin' at him wi' his ain teeth."

"We jist hope that she disnae fa' for a failin' undertaker," Erchie said. "Ah keep tellin' her for tae mairry money. Ah jist hope this Adolph wan has got a few bob."

"Well, he'll be up here this week and you'll be able for tae tell," Tyrone said. "He might be loaded."

Erchie shook his head. "Naw, Ah'm sure Bunty wull have made sure he arrives here sober."

"Naw, Ah meant he might be loaded wi' money. Ye'll be able for tae tell by his gear – know whit Ah mean?" Tyrone was serious.

"Naw, whit dae ye mean?" Erchie said.

"Well, if he turns up here wearin' a golf jaicket ye'll know he hisnae got tuppence," Tyrone said.

"Whit dae ye mean a golf jaicket?" Erchie snapped. "He's comin' for tae pick Bunty up tae take her oot."

"They're goin' tae a fancy dress party," Sadie interrupted.

"Aye, that's mair like it," Erchie said. "He's no' gonny take her for a quick round at Troon – golf jaicket." Erchie spat out the words contemptuously.

"Naw, ye don't understaun'," Tyrone protested. "When Ah said he might turn up wearin' a golf jaicket Ah didnae mean wearin' a jaicket that ye wear for tae play golf in, know whit Ah mean?"

"*Naw!*" Sadie and Erchie said together.

"Ah meant he might show his poverty by wearin' a golf jaicket – wan wi' eighteen holes in it – get it?"

Erchie and Sadie glanced at each other and Sadie threw up her arms.

Tyrone guffawed , pleased with himself.

"Dae ye think Bunty is gonny mairry Herr Adolph?" he asked when he saw his joke was not appreciated.

"God forbid!" Erchie exclaimed.

40

"Ah think if oor Bunty wants tae get merried she'll have for tae go and visit the auld blacksmith," Sadie said.

"She's no' mairryin' a hoarse, is she?" Tyrone asked, screwing up his brows.

"Gretna, Tyrone – she'll hiv for tae elope tae Gretna Green 'cos there's no' a penny comin' intae this hoose since Wurzel Gummidge here got kicked oot o' Shakutis. He is a racist and a bigot," Sadie snapped, glowering at Erchie, who sat nonchalantly pretending to read.

"Is that right, Wurzel?" Tyrone asked."It's no' true, int it no'?"

"Don't you dare call me Wurzel," Erchie exploded. "It is nut true. Ah don't care whit anybody is as long as they're Scottish. "The fact that they fired me has got nothin' tae sae wi' anythin'. But jist you wait. Ah am jist waitin' for the right opportunity for to get ma own back."

"Aye, well you jist get yer skates on and get doon tae that factory and beg if ye hiv tae," Sadie was losing patience.

"Ah wull *nut* beg. It's a matter o' principle, Sadie," Erchie said earnestly. "Every man in this world is allowed for tae go tae the lavvy as he desires. That's a' Ah did and, because Ah was merely obeyin' the call of nature, that wee Nyaff had me fired." Erchie was bitter. "Shakutis have loast a good worker," he added.

"How? Did somebody else leave?" Sadie asked sarcastically. The sarcasm was lost on Erchie.

"Naw, jist me," he said. "*They* wull get me back when *they* come tae *me* and *they* beg Honolable Elchie for to return tae his bench. In the meantime Ah might jist go doon tae the Joab Centre and see if they hiv anythin' for an executive."

"Ur ye no' flyin' a bit high, Erchie?" Tyrone asked. "Ah mean you've got tae hiv a good education for tae be an executive, know whit Ah mean?"

Erchie puckered his lip. "Life has been ma education, Tyrone," he said. "Life!"

"Hiv ye got any Highers, Erchie?" Tyrone inquired.

"Ah never touch drugs, Tyrone," Erchie said.

"Naw, Ah meant O Levels and Highers an' that," Tyrone said.

"*Naebody* in Scotland has got O-Levels, Tyrone," Erchie said, "*Naebody.*"

"Ye mean we're a' plain ignorant, Erchie," Tyrone asked.

41

"Ah do *nut* mean that, Tyrone," Erchie said. "We, in Scotland, do nut hiv O-levels. We hiv O-*Grades* – *Grades*, Tyrone, *Grades* – it's the English that hiv O-*Levels*."

Tyrone beamed broadly. "Geez, Erchie," he whooped, "you hiv jist taught me somethin' Ah never knew."

"Ye mean aboot O-grades and O-levels?" Erchie asked.

"Naw, that your Bunty wore false teeth," Tyrone said.

"If you don't watch yer gub you'll be needin' them as well," Erchie said.

"Would ye like a wee drink, Tyrone?" Sadie said.

Tyrone's eyes lit up. "Oh, aye, thanks, Sadie," he said.

"Well, Ah'm sorry Ah canny gie ye wan since Erm Bender here is noo wan o' the great unemployed. The nearest we get tae liquor in this hoose is a packet o' wine gums," Sadie moaned.

Erchie ruffled his paper. "Aw, shut it," he said.

Suddenly Erchie let out a triumphant yell. Holding up the paper he started doing a jig. Sadie's mouth fell open and Tyrone gaped.

"*Look!*" Erchie cried. "Jist look at that." He waved the paper like a victory banner, all the time dancing with glee.

Sadie's hand came up to her heart. "Oh my God!" she gasped. "Ah thought ye had won the lottery or somethin'. Ah've never heard ye cry wi' happiness so much since ye saw ma maw fa'in doon the stairs."

"This is even better than that," Erchie said through his elation, "a loat better. There *is* a God! It's the answer tae ma prayer, so it is." Erchie thrust the newspaper into Tyrone's hand. "Read that," he cried. "Jist read that —"

Tyrone produced a pair of specs and peered at the paper.

"So, whit am Ah supposed for tae read?" he queried.

"Open yer eyes, dammit," Erchie cried, "Look . . ." he stabbed his finger on the paper.

Tyrone cleared his throat and holding the paper at nose length finally shrugged and handed it back to Erchie.

"Ah canny read!" he said, blushing. "An' Ah can only write ma name."

"Ye can only write 'Tyrone'?" Erchie said in disbelief.

"Only recently hiv Ah started tae write *Tyrone*. For years Ah thought ma name was 'X'."

"Ah'll read this wonderful news," Erchie said with a shrug.
"Noo, listen tae this . . . '*A special exhibition opens today at Glasgow's Art Gallery, in Kelvin Hall. The exhibition . . .*'" Erchie was interrupted by Bunty breezing in. She was bubbling and was either full of the joys of spring or she was full of something.

"Jist me, mammy," she said to Sadie.

Tyrone beamed. "Hello Bunty," he smiled.

Bunty pecked Erchie's cheek. "Daddy . . . Tyrone." Bunty spotted Mrs Thatcher sitting, propped against a chair. "Oh, Ah see we have a distinguished guest!" she exclaimed.

"She's no' real, Bunty, ma da' made her," Tyrone said proudly.

"Yer da', Tyrone?" Bunty asked in admiration. "A Picasso, eh?"

"Naw, but he does pick his nose noo an' again, right enough," Tyrone said.

"Naw, Ah meant he was an artist," Bunty said, hiding a smile.

"Aye he is," Tyrone said.

Sadie was proud of her daughter. She thought how lovely she looked in her cloth curlers although she had taken collection of a hat box that had arrived earlier from a theatrical costumers. Bunty had said it was a wig. So, if she had hired a wig, why was she wearing curlers. Sadie shook her head and shrugged.

"Show Tyrone yer lovely teeth, Bunty," she said.

Bunty put her hand up to her mouth to remove her teeth only to be stopped by Sadie, who nearly had a fit and, quick as a flash, grabbed her wrist to avoid this cosmetic calamity.

"Naw, naw, hen. Ah meant smile for Tyrone – smile."

Bunty smiled broadly, her teeth glinting in the electric light.

"Whit dae ye think o' them, Tyrone, eh?" Sadie said proudly.

Tyrone clicked his tongue. "Beautiful!" he said, dazzled by Bunty's flashing smile.

"They're porcelain," Bunty said proudly.

"Aye, real expensive they wur," Sadie said, her chest inflated. "At night she disnae put them in a gless o' watter at her bedside. She puts them in the display cabinet."

"Did yer boyfriend make them for ye, hen?" Tyrone said, "the wan that was a mechanic?"

"Ex-Boyfriend," Bunty corrected.

"That used tae be ma name – 'X'," Tyrone said. "It's amazin' whit daft people can dae, int it?"

"Whit dae ye mean *daft*?" Sadie snapped. "Ma lovely daughter does *nut* go aboot wi' daft people – no' like her faither."

"Ah thought ye said that Bunty's auld boyfriend was a mental mechanic," Tyrone pouted.

"*Dental,* Tyrone, *Dental,*" Sadie corrected.

"Ach, well, he's in the past," Bunty twittered. "Ah've got a new boyfreen' noo and ye'll meet him when he comes up for tae collect me tae take me tae the fancy-dress party."

"Dae youse go tae the dancin'?" Tyrone asked.

"Oh, aye," Bunty said. "We love goin' tae the disco."

"He disnae make widden legs, does he?" Tyrone asked, a worried expression on his face.

"Or dae the Goose-Step?" Erchie piped up.

"Whit dae ye mean?" Bunty asked, frowning.

"It's nothin' hen," Sadie said. "It's jist that we don't want for ye tae be birlin' roon the dance flair wi' a widden leg jist because ye want tae keep him in a a joab, know whit Ah mean?"

"Naw, Ah don't know whit ye mean," Bunty said.

"Ye're a lovely lassie," Sadie said, "and loyalty can go only so faur. Ah mean yer faither and me was devastated when ye got a' yer teeth pulled so that you could gie yer boyfriend some work. Love has its limits, Bunty and it disnae always run smooth. Sometimes when things urnae goin' right ye must jist grin and bear it – only, in your case that would hiv been difficult. Yer da' and me are jist worried that ye pick the wrang man. Ah mean ye could suddenly find oot wan day that the man that ye love might need a heart transplant. Noo wi' true love it means gien somebody yer heart – but it disnae mean literally, hen. Ye might need it yersel' – right, Tyrone?"

Tyrone nodded. "Ye're dead right, Sadie. Love *is* a funny thing and makes ye blind, so it does." Tyrone went serious and thoughtful.

"You sound like a wee man that's been hurt, Tyrone?" Sadie said sympathetically.

"Ah was," Tyrone said, "Ah was madly in love wi' this lassie and Ah asked her for tae go wi' me on hoaliday tae Paris. We'd been goin' taegether for four years. Well, she clapped her haun's wi' joy and said she'd love tae go and Ah clapped ma hauns as well. Ah said Ah'd make a' the arrangements and Ah got the tickets and Ah asked her for tae gie me her birth certificate so that Ah could get her passport. And see when Ah read it – Ah was shocked. She was nut as young as she made oot tae me tae be."

"Ye mean she was an auld wumman?" Bunty said with some sympathy.

"She was an auld man," Tyrone said sadly.

Erchie and Sadie glanced at each other, a slight smile on their faces.

"Ye mean ye was winchin' for four years an' ye never suspected?" Erchie said, his brows raised to full elevation.

"He had a high-pitched voice," Tyrone said in way of mitigation.

"Ye was aboot for tae tell us somethin' before Bunty came in, Erchie," Sadie said. "Somethin' that was in the paper."

Erchie beamed. "Aye," he said, grinning. "Providence has stepped in through that door for tae answer ma prayers."

"We don't deal wi' the Providence," Sadie said. "We deal wi' the Co-op."

"Ah am nut talkin' aboot insurance," Erchie said. "Well, no' in that wey."

The topic of conversation was too boring for Bunty. "Ah'll away and try oan ma wig for the big night," she said, leaving the room.

"So, whit's this a' aboot?" Sadie asked, curiously.

"It's ma opportunity for tae get ma own back at Shakutis – and especially that wee Nyaff," Erchie said with glee.

"You've got it in for that wee gaffer , so ye hiv, hiven't ye?"

Sadie thought her husband was blowing things out of all proportion. He was looking for a scapegoat – and excuse.

"It's *him* that had it in for me ever since the first day Ah started. Jist because Ah smoked," Erchie protested.

"Whit makes ye think that?" Sadie asked suspiciously.

"It happened that very first day," Erchie began. "It was the fateful day when oor animosity began. Ah was dying for a fag and went intae the lavvy. Ah'd jist sat doon and lit ma fag and was jist contented for tae sit there and puff away – that's a'."

"An' he took umbrage at that?" Sadie said.

"He did – mind ye he was sittin' on the pan at the time," Erchie said with a straight face.

45

Before Sadie could say a word, Tyrone interrupted. "Right," he said, "C'mon, whit was a' the excitement aboot in the paper?

"Jist listen tae this," Erchie said, his voice quivering with excitement. He ruffled the paper and began to read ... " *'Glasgow Art Galleries is exhibiting a priceless collection of Japanese artifacts, sculptures and paintings. The exhibition is being sponsored by the Glasgow-based Shakutis company . The most valuable exhibit is that of a Samurai Warrior on horseback and this is the first time the collection has been allowed outside Japan and Shakutis have it insured for ten million pounds. It's presence in Glasgow is due to the persistance of Shakutis Chairman Mr Wullie Nagazumi, whose Japanese mother was Aggie McGeachie, from Govan. He persuaded the Nippon government to allow the collection to be shown in Glasgow because of his mother's connection with the city and to foster culture and social relations with its citizens. Mr Nagazumi has guaranteed his government the safety of the collection. Accompanying the Exhibition is the world famous Japanese State Theatre company'.*" Erchie threw up arms in delight. "Whit aboot that, then?" he cried.

"Whit aboot it?" Sadie said, wondering what dastardly deed her husband had in mind.

"Dae ye no' see?" Erchie cried in frustration. "If anythin' happens tae that exhibition it would be a helluva embarrassment for Shakutis. Their name would be mud back hame in Japan. In fact Auld Nagazumi would probably hiv tae commit Hari-Kari."

"He used tae be in' the cowboy pictures," Tyrone said.

"Who? Nagazumi?" Erchie asked, drawing his brows together.

"Naw – Harry Carey," Tyrone said, "He was in a loat o' pictures wi' John Wayne – a great auld actor!"

"That's no' whit we're talkin' aboot ya wee idiot. Hari-Kari is a ritual where they kneel doon and stick a sword intae their belly – it's a wey o' committin' suicide."

"Imagine callin' it efter a cowboy," Tyrone said, puzzled.

"And don't tell me you think somethin's gonny happpen tae that exhibition that wull make Mr Naggyi-hoarsy or whitever his name is get oot his Wilkinson Sword?" Sadie looked worried.

"Ye can bet on it, hen," Erchie said with a smug expression.

"So, whit day suits ye?" Sadie asked.

"Whit dae ye mean, whit days suits me?" Erchie asked .

"For me visitin' ye – in Barlinnie," Sadie said seriously.

"Away ye go," Erchie cried. "No way Ah'm Ah goin' tae Barlinnie."

"Quite right, Erchie," Tyrone said. "Ye'll probably get sent tae Tenko."

"Don't haver, ya wee idiot," Erchie scolded. "Besides we shoap at Azda."

"Whit's that got tae dae wi' bein' sent tae Tenko?" Tyrone said, puzzled.

"Oh, Ah thought ye said Tesco," Erchie said.

"Well, ye're jist askin' for trouble," Sadie said, "and hell mend ye."

"So ye ur," Tyrone agreed.

"You shut yer wee face," Erchie snapped, "Ah know whit Ah'm daein'. By the time Ah'm finished wi' Shakutis Nagazumi wull be honing his samurai sword."

"Can Mr Nagazumi's sword talk?" Tyrone was curious.

"Whit ur ye talkin' aboot ya wee idiot?" Erchie said.

"Well, you said Mr Nagazumi wull be 'phonin' his sword," Tyrone said innocently.

"*Honing*, ya clown, *honin'* – it means sharpenin' it till it's razor sherp – nothin' like your mind – understaun'?"

"So, whit's on *your* mind?" Sadie said, standing defiantly with her arms folded.

"Tyrone an' me ur goin' for tae pay that exhibition a wee visit, so we ur."

"Whit for?" Sadie asked, narrowing her eyes.

"Revenge, hen – revenge," Erchie said with a satisfied grin.

"Ah don't like exhibitions," Tyrone said. "Ah wance went tae an exhibition and ended up in the Royal Infirmary wi' two black eyes."

"Whit kinda exhibition was it?" Erchie asked, puzzled.

"A boxin' wan," Tyrone said, "Ah was jist sittin' there in the crowd and this bloke asked if anybody wanted for tae make ten quid an' Ah put ma haun' up. Well, he invited me tae step up and join him and when Ah did this bloke stepped up as well and gave me a tankin'. So, Ah don't go tae exhibitions noo."

"Well, ye're goin' tae this wan," Erchie commanded.

Tyrone looked to Sadie for support but she knew that no matter what she said Erchie was determined to make a fool of himself. She gave Tyrone a sympathetic smile.

"Whit ur we goin' tae see?" Tyrone asked, knowing he was flogging a dead horse.

"This," Erchie said with a flourish.

He pointed to the colour picture printed across four columns in the paper.

"Who is it – The Lone Ranger?" Tyrone asked, looking intently at the picture.

"It's a Samurai Warrior mounted on his hoarse," Erchie said.

Tyrone screwed up his nose. This was all beyond him. What exactly *was* in Erchie's mind? Art did not interest him and he thought the Tate Gallery was a sugar factory. The only art he did appreciate were the drawings of Desperate Dan and Pansy Potter. And what exactly *was* a Samurai Warrior and what was his pal, Erchie's, interest in it? If Shakutis wanted to sponsor an exhibition, why not? It was only right that we get to know others' cultures. It was only recently that he had appreciated a can of spaghetti and suddenly he wanted to know everything Italian – patricularly Sophia Loren's address. He had heard of the Elgin Marbles and wondered what was so special about them. He had played with his 'jories' for many years of his childhood in the tenement streets of Glasgow, so why the big fuss over the boys playing in the comparatively posh streets of Elgin. There were many things he didn't understand.

Tyrone furrowed his brows. "Tell me, Erchie," he said. "Whit exactly *is* a Samurai Warrior?"

Erchie cleared his throat. "Well – er," he began, "er – ye know when sojers ur staunin' there a' lined up for battle jist waitin' for the command for to advance?"

Tyrone nodded. "Aye, Ah saw that in *The Charge O' The Light Brigade*," he said.

"Well – er," Erchie hesitated, "maist o' the warriors, that's another name for sojers, Tyrone, obey the order withoot question and charge forward wi' fixed bayonets but Samurai haud back too frightened – see whit Ah mean? Maist go but Samurai are reluctant and stey put."

Tyrone was impressed by Erchie's superior knowledge. He never knew his own father was a Samurai Warrior. He was just a boy during World War Two and his father was away in the army

He remembered tugging his mother's sleeve and asking where his daddy was only to be told that he was in Jankers. He thought that was a foreign country where the war was at its fiercest. It was many years later before he understood what Jankers was. So, it would seem, his father was a Samurai.

"So, whit has that Samurai in the Kelvingrove Gallery got tae dae wi' us?" he asked.

"Because," Erchie said, "you and me, Tyrone, are gonny steal that Samurai – their maist precious exhibit. Nagazumi's face wull go redder than a Lanarkshire tomato. He wull never be able for to set feet in Japan ever again." Erchie had a smug expression.

"You ur *nut* bringin' a hoarse intae this hoose," Sadie snapped.

Tyrone nodded in agreement. "Sadie's right, Erchie," he said, "ye've nae room for a hoarse. It would've been different if he'd been oan a Shetland Pony – but no a big hoarse. Ah hiv never seen a hoarse in a hoose – except for the wan ma maw had for hingin' her waashin' on."

"Don't be so stupit, stupit," Erchie said. "We wull not pinch the hoarse – jist the man on toap."

"Aw, that's a'right, then," Tyrone said, relieved. He did not like the idea of carrying a large horse down Sauchiehall Street.

"It is *nut* all right," Sadie snapped. "Ah do nut want a strange Japanese man in ma hoose. Ther's nae place tae put him."

"We wull find a place," Erchie said, "*He* is central tae ma plan."

Erchie was adamant and Sadie knew it would be useless to argue.

"It's no' like he'll be eatin yer food or anythin', Sadie," Tyrone volunteered.

"Thanks, Tyrone," Erchie said, glad of an ally.

"Ye think ye're jist gonny walk intae the Kelvingrove Galleries and walk oot wi' Hirohito there, dae ye – jist like that?" Sadie said through gritted teeth.

"There's a wey," Erchie said, "there's *always* a wey."

"Sadie's got a point, Erchie," Tyrone said."How ur ye gonny dae it?"

"You'll see," Erchie said."Noo, furst, get oot that packet o'quick-dryin' starch, Sadie and fill the bath."

"Whit for?" Sadie asked, puzzled.

"Ah want ye tae keep Mrs Thatcher in a sittin' position – jist like she is noo on that chair – and dip her in the starch for a few minutes. Then hing her up."

"A loat o' people waanted tae dae that," Tyrone chuckled.

"Tae dry on the pulley," Erchie added.

Sadie shrugged. Just another one of her husband's daft ideas. She prepared the bath and sprinkled enough starch in for the operation in hand. Then she took the paper effigy of the former Prime Minister and dipped her into the starch.

★   ★   ★

One hour later the effigy was hanging from the pulley and an hour after that she was brought down. Sadie carried her into the room where Erchie and Tyrone waited.

"There ye ur," Sadie said, "Dead stiff – jist like you on a Setturday night."

Erchie ignored his wife's comments. Sadie placed Tyrone's old man's masterpiece on an easy chair and there it sat, printed all over with the latest news topped by a smiling face.

"Perfect!" Erchie exclaimed.

"So, whit next?" Tyrone said.

"You go in and bring oot yer faither's wheelchair – but make sure he's no' in it."

Tyrone left the room and, checking that his father was comfortable in his bed, happy with his origami, he pushed the chair out and into Erchie's house.

"Right!" Erchie said, "Noo, we place Mrs Thatcher in the chair and cover her legs wi' a blanket."

With Tyrone's help, he carefully lifted the effigy from the chair and placed it in the wheelchair. A blanket was fetched and placed over the knees.

"Gie's that auld hat you wore at Granny McGillicuddy's funeral, Sadie." Sadie fetched the hat which was placed on the effigy's head. Erchie stepped back and surveyed his work.

"Beautiful!" he said. "Right, Ty, c'mon, you and me and Mrs Thatcher here are goin a wee walk."

"Everybody'll know that that's no' ma da," Tyrone protested.

"How?" Erchie asked.

"That big smile. Ma da' disnae smile – ever."

"How's that?" Erchie asked, "Nae joy in his heart?"

"Nae teeth in his mooth," Tyrone said.

"Naebody'll notice," Erchie said. "C'mon."

The two men man-handled the chair through the door and down the stairs and out into the street.

"See youse oan visitin' day," Sadie hollered from the window. Erchie gave her a dismissive wave and, with Mrs Thatcher smiling broadly, they trundled on down the street, turning towards Sauchiehall Street and the Kelvingrove Art Galleries.

CHAPTER TWO

THE TWO MEN COLLECTED MORE THAN TWO POUNDS IN COINS AS they shoved the wheelchair along. As Guy Fawkes night was just a few days away the Glasgow citizens reckoned they were a couple of old soldiers down in their luck and, as all Glaswegians have pity for those down at heel, they dipped into their pockets. Erchie was forming an idea that this might be a lucrative ploy to consider for the future. But he knew Sadie would never allow it. She would be shame-faced if she thought her husband was out begging. He could sing around the back courts, or what was left of them in the new modelled Glasgow, if he wanted but no direct begging. That was too blatant

It was a fair walk from Bridgeton to the Kelvingrove Galleries but it would be worth it. Besides, this was the only way they could travel if Erchie's military style action was to be achieved.

Not many people paid attention to the duo after they left the precincts of Bridgeton. Passing by a conservative club up town, the blue-uniformed doorman snapped to attention and saluted smartly. He was rewarded by a broad smile – paper thin, but broad.

Soon they arrived at the imposing red-stone building that was Glasgow's pride. There was little activity which pleased Erchie. They pushed the chair up to the front door and entered the magnificent gallery. Erchie had covered up his passenger as best he could and now, only Sadie's hat was peeking through. The security man at the foyer nodded and in answer to Erchie's question as to the whereabouts of the great Samurai Warrior, set him off in the right direction.

Tyrone was mesmerised by the beauty of the art around him as the made their way to their goal. "Oh, look," he cried. "There's a wumman wi' nae claeths oan."

"That's nut unusual in this district, Tyrone," Erchie said.

They followed the printed signs that read *This way to the*

Shakutis Art Exhibition and their jaws dropped as they turned into the great hall and saw the magnificent charger with the Samurai Warrior astride it.

"Aw, wid ye look at that!" Erchie exclaimed in awe.

"Ye wid think it was alive," Tyrone said, his mouth open.

"Ah sometimes wonder if *you're* alive," Erchie said.

"Whit dae we dae noo, then?" Tyrone asked.

"You go oot there an' kid on ye're lookin' at pictures and keep that security man busy."

"Aye, Ah like lookin' at them pictures," Tyrone said.

He left and sauntered into the foyer. stopping and gazing at pictures on the way. Attracting the security man's attention, he said, "That's some paintin', that wan o' that helluva ugly lookin' man. Who painted that?"

"That's a mirror, sir," the man said.

"Oh!" Tyrone uttered and continued with his tour.

Erchie was finding it a struggle to get the warrior down from his horse but, pulling a chair over, he finally managed to reach and remove it. There were no other visitors around to see this nefarious sting in progress and Erchie blessed his luck. He struggled to replace the figure on the horse with his Mrs Thatcher cut-out. Finally done, he stepped back and surveyed his handiwork. The origami effigy sat perfectly astride the horse. Erchie smiled. He was pleased with himself. The Samurai, now snug in the wheelchair, was covered by the blanket and ready to be taken away to its new home, in Bridgeton. As he pushed the wheelchair towards the door a class of school children were shown in by their teacher.

"This, children, is a ferocious Samurai Warrior," the teacher said, pointing out the exhibit."

"Please miss, he looks awful like Mrs Thatcher," one wee girl said, tugging the teacher's sleeve.

"That, ya wee trollop is a Samurai Warrior who just looks like Mrs Thatcher."

"Sorry Miss," the girl said.

"That's all right. It was the teeth that fooled you."

Erchie walked out of the building without being challenged and was joined by Tyrone who was glad to be out of the building after being shadowed by that security guard.

* * *

Sadie paced the floor at home, chewing her nails. Erchie had done some stupid things during their married life but never anything like this. Shakutis had been good to them and Erchie had a fair wage. But he was thrawn' and, to her mind, an amateur racist. Shakutis employed hundreds of local people and all were grateful for the work – all except Erchie, that is. But Erchie would always find something to complain about.

Sadie had noticed the writing pad and biro pen lying on top of the sideboard and wondered who Erchie was writing to. This was against the grain for Erchie never wrote. It taxed his brain too much, Sadie reckoned. The pen and paper was not used by Bunty for Bunty was into caligraphy and used nothing but pen and ink. A ball point to Bunty was like a surgeon using a knife and fork for a delicate operation. So, Erchie had to be the phantom writer – but to whom?

Sadie hoped that he wouldn't change his mind and bring the horse with him. Erchie did things on impulse and if he saw his opportunity, might just take the lot. Sadie was worried and kept glancing towards the door.

She jumped with a start as she heard a loud clatter coming from the stairs. Suddenly the door flew open as Erchie juggled and cajoled the wheelchair through the door pushing it to the middle of the room. With a flourish he whipped off the blanket.

"*Voila!*" he cried

The expressionless warrior sat staring straight ahead. Only a row of gleaming teeth, straight as a row of tombstones betrayed his ferocity.

"Oh my God!" she said. "He looks that real. Ye didnae bring his hoarse, did ye?"

"That hoarse is a very special hoarse, so it is," Erchie said miffed.

"Ah don't care if it's Shergar," Sadie snapped. "You ur nut bringin' it in here."

"It would be good tae hiv if ye're gonny plant totties," Tyrone piped up.

"Ah'll plant you if ye don't shut up," Sadie said.

54

"Ah was only tryin' for tae help," Tyrone said, hurt.

"Well, ye don't need for tae worry, hen, Ah left the hoarse there wi' Mrs Thatcher oan toap," Erchie said.

Sadie was relieved. The house was crowded when they had a dog – Mitzi, a little King Charles spaniel. A horse in the house would have been intolerable. She hoped Erchie was finding sense.

"So whit ur we gonny dae wi' Sushi here?" Sadie said, jabbing her thumb towards the warrior.

"He's a' right where he is," Erchie said.

Ah see the writin' pad an' pen lyin' oot," Sadie said. "Who've ye been writin' tae? Efter a joab Ah hope."

"Naw, it's part two of ma plan," Erchie said.

"Is Yammymoto here part wan?"

"He is. They ur gonny be sorry they ever heard o' me," Erchie said.

"Ah'm sorry Ah ever heard o' ye," Sadie snapped.

"Whit is Plan Two, Erchie?" Tyrone asked, screwing up his nose. "Ah don't even know whit Plan Wan was."

"Plan Two, Tyrone," Erchie began talking very precisely, "is that Ah intend suein' Shakutis for plenty."

Sadie threw up her arms. "Huh!" she cried. "*You* suein' *them*? They should be suein *you* for shirkin'. So, whit ur ye gonny sue them for?"

"For the terrible disease Ah caught workin' in their slave camp," Erchie said determinedly.

"Whit disease did *you* catch?" Sadie asked, puzzled.

"Aw, Erchie, Ah'm sorry for tae hear that," Tyrone said sympathetically, "Ah didnae know ye had caught a disease or Ah wid've steyed ten yards away frae ye. Whit disease is it. Yella Fever?"

"Whitever it is it isnae affectin' his muscles anyway. His elbow is still bendin' as usual," Sadie said facetiously.

"As faur as they ur concerned Ah hiv caught a very unusual disease because of the work Ah was daen in that place."

"And whit work were you daein'?" Sadie asked suspiciously. "As faur as Ah know ye were never oot the lavvy hivin' a puff. In fact the smoke that came oot their big lum had nothin' tae dae wi' the work there. It was you sittin' in the cludge puffin' away, so it was."

"That is nut true," Erchie said. "Ah only went in durin' ma break and had wan fag."

"Wan o' they four-foot long wans ye roll yersel'?" Sadie said.

"Aw, come aff it," Erchie said.

"Aye, right, so whit is this disease you hiv contracted?" Sadie asked curiously.

"Shrink-itis," Erchie said flatly.

"*Shrink-itis*?" Tyrone and Sadie cried together.

"A very terrible disease," Erchie said.

"Ah think Ah know whit ye mean," Sadie said. "It's a contageous disease that's nae stranger tae this hoose. Ma wages took that disease. They shrank an' shrank every week until noo when they've disappeared a' the gether."

"Ye're gonny hiv mair money than ye know whit tae dae wi', hen, when Ah win ma case," Erchie said grinning.

"Who did ye write tae?" Sadie asked.

"Ah wrote tae the heid bummer, Nagazumi, himsel'," Erchie said. "He has only met me wance but he'll soon be dyin' or tae get acquainted wi' yours truly."

"Whit a treat he's in for," Sadie said with sarcasm.

Erchie ignored Sadie's facetious comment. Turning to Tyrone, he said. "And, as for you ya wee idiot, ye do nut get Yella Fever in Glesca – Green Fever or Blue Fever, aye, but definitely nut Yella Fever."

"A'right, then," Tyrone said, "tell us aboot this disease ye've got. Whit does it dae tae ye?"

"Well," Erchie began, dramatically illustrating with his hands coming closer and closer together, "ye shrink and shrink and go oan shrinkin' until ye disappear a' the gether – it's horrible."

"You're no' a' there anywey," Sadie said.

"Ah hiv never heard o' it before," Tyrone said.

"Ah'm no' surprised you hivnae heard o' it," Erchie said. "You think mumps is a cartoon character, yae idiot. *Shrink-itis*, Tyrone, is a disease prevalent tae Africa. Ye don't normally get it in Glesca. It's another Japanese import, Tyrone. Pygmies in Africa were wance seven-feet-two and a hauf inches tall. Then wan day a Jap missionary wandered intae their jungle camp an' they ate him. Frae that moment they started for tae shrink until they were dead wee."

56

"Ur you sure?" Tyrone was sceptical.

"They were wance admired for their skill in huntin' elephants but jist efter wan plateful o' Jap missionary they were reduced tae huntin' rabbits and as time went oan – mice," Erchie said convincingly.

"That's a' very well, Smarty Pants, but jist tell me wan thing how ur you gonny convince them that you ur shrinkin shoart o' cuttin' aff yer legs?" Sadie stood, adamant, arms folded.

"Dae ye think oor doactor would gie me a line?" Erchie asked narowing his eyes.

"Doactor McKenzie might be daft but he's no' blind," Sadie said, referring to the family GP.

Suddenly there was a loud cry from next door. It was a yell of triumph but Tyrone almost jumped out of his skin.

"Ma da'!" he cried, "Ah keep forgettin' aboot him."

"Ye'd better go in an' see whits wrang," Sadie said concern in her voice.

Tyrone left hurriedly.

"Ah hope nothin's wrang," Sadie said.

"He's probably drapped a stitch or somethin'," Erchie replied.

"Whit dae ye think Mr Nagazumi wull dae when he gets yer letter?" Sadie asked.

"He'll panic and send me a cheque by the next post," Erchie said confidently.

Sadie was about to reply but a loud yell from next door made her jump. Tyrone came rushing in holding a life-size effigy of Marilyn Monroe, expertly cut out from the pink *Financial Times*.

"Look whit ma da's been daein," Tyrone cried with pride.

"Lookin' at that," Erchie said, "wan question comes tae ma mind."

"An' whit's that?" Tyrone asked.

"Where did *you* get haud o' the *Financial Times*?"

"Ah picked it up at the dentist's when Ah went tae pick up ma da's teeth," Tyrone said.

"And he decided tae make Marilyn Monroe wi' it, eh?" Sadie said, admiring the work that had gone into it.

"Aye, it was either wan Mailyn Monroe or six or seven Ronnie Corbetts," Tyrone said proudly.

"That's a nice, smiling face he's stuck oan," Sadie said, taking the art work from Tyrone, "Here," she said, "we'll let her sit there." She placed Marilyn on an easy chair, her legs dangling over the edge.

Sadie and Tyrone stood back and surveyed the old man's handiwork.

"Aye, she looks right at hame sittin' there," Sadie said. Tyrone nodded his approval..

The sudden shrill of the telephone rooted everybody to their spot. Nobody made a move to answer the persistent ringing. Each wondering who could be at the other end of the line. Finally Sadie hesitantly picked up the receiver.

"Er – hello –" she said, almost in a whisper. "Yes – uh-huh –" Erchie and Tyrone stood and watched with bated breath.

"Y – yes, he – he's here – uh-hu." Sadie held out the receiver.

"It's for you," she said to Erchie.

"Wh . . . who is it?" Erchie stammered.

"Mr Nagazumi," Sadie said.

"Oh, God he's received ma letter," Erchie gasped, "Er . . . er . . . tell him Ah'm no' in," he said.

"Ah've already telt him ye *ur* in," Sadie said, jabbing the phone towards him.

"Then tell him the phone's oan tap o' the sideboard and Ah canny reach it," Erchie said, shaking a little and unprepared for a personal telephone call from the Chairman of the Board.

"Don't be stupit," Sadie snapped, "Ah'm no' tellin' him ye canny reach the phone."

"Aye, ye're better for tae answer it, Erchie," Tyrone piped in. "He might want tae know if ye want yer money in a postal order or a cheque or that – know whit Ah mean?"

Erchie drew his eyebows together. "Maybe he wants for tae settle oot o' court," he said.

"Aye, maybe he wants tae gie the money oot o' court or maybe in that wee pub roon' the coarner frae the courthoose," Tyrone said.

Erchie threw him a contemptuous look.

"Ye's baith livin' in cloud cuckoo land," Sadie said. "Mr Nagazumi is no' gonny gie you wan penny before he's had a doactor examinin' ye frae heid tae toe."

"Aye, ye're probably right," Erchie said. "So whit dae ye think he wants?"

Sadie removed her cupped hand from the mouthpiece.

"Aye, Mr Nagazumi," she said. "Here he is for to talk to you himsel'." She handed the phone to Erchie, who cleared his throat.

"Hello – ye – this *is* three-feet-two tall Erchie Hunter speaking from the top of a pianna stool. Aye, of cooorse Ah know who you ur, you ur the slave driver Ah hiv been workin' for before Ah was suddenly struck doon and Ah do mean *doon*. So, you got ma letter, eh? Of coorse Ah'm serious. Ah get hauf fare oan the bus noo and Ah've loast a lot o' weight ma dug keeps wantin' tae bury me in the back gairden."

"It's no' the only wan," Sadie said.

"Believe me if ye like. Ah am not a comedian although some folk hiv likened me tae Big Ronnie Corbett. Right jist dae that – anytime ye like. Cheers."

Erchie slammed the phone down and, with a broad smile, turned toward Sadie and Tyrone.

"That telt him," he said smugly.

"So, whit did he say he's gonny dae?" Sadie inquired.

"How much is he gonny gie ye?" Tyrone asked.

"He didnae mention money, no' yet, anywey. He's comin' roon ta see me," Erchie said. Then, realising the implications of those words, slapped his forehead with the palm of his hand.

"Oh, God!" he cried "Whit'll Ah dae whit –?" Erchie scurried around the room in a panic like a cat with its tail on fire.

"That's the ba' up in the slates, then, intit?" Sadie said.

"Want me tae go an' get it Sadie?" Tyrone said.

"Get whit?" Sadie asked.

"Yer ba'," Tyrone said. "Ah mean it could be dangerous. It could loosen some slates that could fa' doon oan somebody's heid."

"Ah think you've got a few slates missin'," Erchie said.

"Ah'm only tryin' tae help," Tyrone said, hurt.

"Ah know ye ur, Ty," Sadie said, patting his shoulder, "We're a' a bit upset the noo. So," she said, turning to Erchie, "whit ur ye gonny dae noo, eh?" Sadie had a tone of *I told you so*.

"Well, Ah'm telt auld Nagazumi's very shoart-sighted. He

wears jeely-jaur specs. He might no' notice," Erchie said, trying to convince himself.

"He'd need tae be stone blind no' tae see through your daft ploy," Sadie said.

"Ah'm no' so sure," Erchie went on. "He's that shoart-sighted, Ah'm tellin' ye, that Ah remember wan time Ah had occasion for tae go up tae his oaffice on behalf of the work force for to complain aboot the doors oan the toilets."

"Whit aboot them?" Sadie asked.

"We wanted them," Erchie said, "same as the wummen."

"So whit's that got tae dae wi' him bein' shoart sighted?"

"The first thing he asked me was did Ah like dugs? When Ah telt him Ah did he stuck oot his chist and showed me a picture that was oan his desk. "Me tae," he said. "This is a picture of honorable dug, Mitzi, back hame in honorable hoose, in Tokyo."

"Aye, very nice, but whit's that got tae dae wi' his shoart-sightedness?" Sadie asked, puzzled.

"It was an elephant," Erchie said.

"Och, ye're daft," Sadie pooh-poohed.

"*Me* daft?" Erchie cried. "Ah that knew it was an elephant."

"Aye, well, Ah still think ye're on a sticky wicket," Sadie said.

"Aye, well, we'll see. Ah hiv a contingency plan and Ah'd better get goin' an start puttin' it intae practice." Erchie sounded confident.

"Whit aboot him?" Sadie said, jabbing a thumb towards the sitting Samurai Warrior.

"Aye, he's a problem," Erchie said, stroking his chin. Then, snapping his fingers, he cried, "Open the windae!"

"Ye're no' gonny throw him oot the windae, Erchie, ur ye?" Tyrone sounded genuinely concerned for the lifeless warrior.

"Don't be daft. Here, gie me a haun'."

Sadie opened the window in the room and Erchie and Tyrone manhandled the dummy over. Then Erchie placed the sitting figure out on to the sill, its legs dangling into the room. Before closing the window down he stuck a chamois in its right hand. Standing back, he nodded, satisfied.

"There noo," he said. "Naebody'll gie him a second look. Right, come oan, Tyrone, we're goin' oot. Plan Two comin' up."

"Where ur ye goin'?" Sadie asked.

"We'll be back soon. You entertain Nagazumi if he shows up. Oaffer him a drink. Hiv we any saké in the hoose?"

"Oh, aye, bucketsful," Sadie said with sarcasm.

"Oh, gonny gie me some, Sadie," Tyrone cried.

"Efter, Tyrone, efter," Erchie said, pushing him through the door.

Sadie stood in front of the window and stared at her guest.

"You make a good joab o' they windaes noo," she said. She walked across the room and flopped into an easy chair and let her mind wander. "Aw, where is it a' gonny end?" she thought. Erchie wisnae always like this. This Mr Nagazumi canny be the dumplin' Erchie paints him. He was shrewd enough tae see through him and have him fired. Erchie says he didnae dae anything tae get the sack. That's probably right. He was in there tae work and he wisnae daen anythin'. Ah wonder if he should see a lawyer or a psychiatrist. Maybe he *should* see a shrink, efter a' that's whit he's daein' accordin' tae him. He was a different man when we first got married. Bunty was jist two at the time. He used tae take ma haun' and squeeze it – in the mangle. But that was jist his wey. He didnae mean anything by it. Naw, Mr Nagazumi isnae daft. Any other boss would've ordered Erchie for tae appear in front o' him at the factory. But Mr Nagazumi wants tae keep Erchie well away frae the factory 'cos he knows that wance Erchie's on the factory premises he'll hiv everybody oot on strike. So, shrewdly, *he* is comin' here and Ah canny blame him. Sadie relaxed back on the chair and sighed deeply. Her thoughts were shattered by the phone ringing breaking the silence.

"Hello, The Hunter residence," she said – "Oh, it's you, Erchie? Where ur ye? Ye're no' up at the Royal Infirmary hivin' yer legs amputated, ur ye? Me? Naw, Ah'm in oor hoose – jist me and Marilyn Monroe and the windae cleaner. Naw, he hasnae arrived yet – Aye, Ah'll keep him occupied mair than he's daein' for you – aye, Ah'll put oan a record o' the *Ying Tong Song* – and you get hame here pronto – if ye can still walk, that is."

Sadie had just cradled the phone when it rang once again.

"Hello – oh, it's yersel', Bunty," she said. "Ye'll no' be in for yer tea? A'right – naw, Ah'm waitin' for Mr Nagazumi comin' up for tae see yer da'. Adolph thinks yer faither's a racist – naw, of coorse no' – did he no' go oot his wey for tae help Mr Singh frae the coarner paper shoap get back tae Bangladesh for his daughter's weddin'? – Noo, is that the work o' a racist? He knew Mr Singh couldnae afford the fare so he reported him as an illegal immigrant and got him deported – it's jist Japs and Germans he disnae like – he's jealous o' them."

A loud knock on the door made Sadie jump.

"Oh, Ah'll hiv tae go, hen," she cried, "there's somebody at the door."

Sadie cradled the phone, smoothed down her 'peenie', had a quick glance at herself in the wall mirror, buffing her hair up. She stood, hand on the door handle, cleared her throat and opened the door.

Mr Nagazumi, a small portly man wearing very thick-lensed glasses removed his bowler hat and bowed reverently.

"Honourable Mr Hunter?" he asked.

"Naw, Ah'm dishonourable *Missus* Hunter," Sadie said.

"Lovely lady does herself an injustice," Nagazumi said.

"Come in," Sadie said and guided him to a chair facing Marilyn Monroe. "Sit doon," Sadie said and saw that the old man was settled comfortably in the chair.

"Very pleased to meet you, Ah-So," Nagazumi said.

"Ye don't hiv tae be rude, Mr Nagazumi," Sadie said, frowning.

"Not being rude, honourable wumman," the man said, "Ah-So, is well known Japanese phrase."

"Ah thought ye were callin' me a rude name," Sadie said.

"No. no. Missy. Rude names kept for your husband," Nagazumi said. "Him here?"

Sadie shook her head. "He's oot – but he'll no' be long,"Sadie said.

"Him no' be long because him short, eh? A good joke, no?" Nagazumi chuckled.

"Aye, right enough," Sadie said, a worried expression on her face.

"He say he is shrinking, Mrs Wumman," Nagazumi said, furrowing his eyebrows. "You think he is shrinking?"

"Well, let's put it this wey," Sadie said. "He used tae go tae Ralph Slater's for his claeths – but noo —"

"Where he go noo?" Nagazumi asked.

62

"Mothercare," Sadie said.

Mr Nagazumi hid a smile. He admired a woman who would stand by her husband no matter how ludicrous his situation.

"Honorable doctors say his shrinking not possible. They say maybe just his heid shrinking. Him just daft."

"Aye, well ma Erchie's daft the right wey," Sadie said angrily. "He used tae come intae this hoose every Friday and haun' me mair than two hunner pounds wages he picked up frae Martin's Leather Works, in Heron Street."

"So, what so smart about that?" Nagazumi said.

"He didnae work there." Sadie stood erect and defiant.

Mr Nagazumi smiled. "Where is honourable husband noo?" he asked.

Sadie cleared her throat. "He's away tae Saxones to purchase a pair of platform shoes," she said in her best Kelvinside accent.

"Ah, now you try to pull wool over these old eyes, eh?" Nagazumi said with a wry smile.

"Ah could never get it ower yer specs," Sadie said.

"Mrs Wumman must think me came up the Yangtse in bike," Nagazumi said. "Your husband trying it on. You say he give you wages from factory where he no' work. Well, he no' work in my factory either."

"Oh aye he did," Sadie said, "He worked in Shakutis for weeks and weeks."

"He come to factory for weeks and weeks but he no' work," Nagazumi said. "Hauf the time he hidin' in honourable lavvy – smokin'."

"Aye, well Ah know ma Erchie likes his wee puff."

"Wee Puff?" Nagazumi cried, "Twice we had honourable Fire Brigade screaming up to oor door. He is no' getting job back and can shrink into honourable sunset as far as I am concerned."

"Would ye no' consider takin' him back in a less active capacity, Mr Nagazumi?" Sadie's tone was softer. She not only want Erchie to find a job, she wanted him to be reinstated at Shakutis which paid well and was near at hand.

"Any less active capacity and he would be a statue," Nagazumi said. "He was the only employee of mine who, at recreation time in factory garden, dugs came up to him an' cocked their leg. Naw, canny think of any less active capacity."

Sadie smiled to herslf. "Oh, you are a wan," she said, digging him in the ribs.

"No, no, me no' a wan. Wan is honourable brother-in-law." Shito Wan. Now, you tell me, where is your dishonourable husband?"

"He's probably in the pub hopin' for a wee lift," Sadie said.

"Hopin' for a wee lift?" Nagazumi said.

"Aye, he's probably walked up tae the bar hopin' that somebody wull gie him a wee lift oan tae the stool," Sadie said.

"He go out and leave you alone, Mrs Hunter except for honourable window cleaner there and this very charming and silent lady in pink dress?" With that he stood up and strolled over to the window and narrowing his eyes, peered at the figure outside with chamois in hand.

"He look like my brother-in-law, Shito Wan but a dead slow worker. He still on that wan pane – ha-ha—, get it , *wan* pane." Nagazumi laughed heartily.

" Very funny," Sadie said without a smile. "C'mon sit doon on that nice comfortable easy chair, or wid ye prefer sittin' oan the flair like youse dae in Japan?"

"No' all Japanese people sit on floors in their homes, Mrs Hunter, some don't," Nagazumi said.

"Who disnae?" Sadie asked.

"Wans wi' chairs in the hoose," Nagazumi said.

Sadie blushed. She found the old gentleman just that – an old gentleman and a shrewd one, too. Erchie was hitting his head against a brick wall and would come out of all this badly bruised, she thought.

"Ah'm sorry Erchie is suein' you, Mr Nagazumi," Sadie found herself saying.

"Just be glad we no' sueing *him*," Nagazumi said.

"Er – aye – er – would you like a wee cuppa tea?" Sadie said stammering.

"You very kind," he said.

Sadie left to prepare the tea leaving Nagazumi sitting facing Tyrone's old man's Marilyn Monroe masterpiece. The old man cleared his throat.

"You very quiet wumman, hen," Nagazumi said, addressing the cut-out. "You a saint amongst women – and with simple tastes, too. Most women go to honourable Marks and Spencers or Laura Ashley for their claeths, you obviously go to WH Smith's. Ah hiv heard Glesca girls like wear printed froacks but that's ridiculous. Glesca is wonderful city – just like Tokyo but with grafitti. They have taken to Japanese people – even adopting some of our names. The Big *Yin*, for instance, and, *Mo* Johnstone – *Yin* and *Mo* good Japan names. Youse-a even call your dram of whisky in honour of Japanese brother the Wee *Nip*, eh?

Sadie enterd with a tray. She placed a cup of tea down in front of her guest.

"Would ye like a Garibaldi Mr Nagazumi?" Sadie asked

"Ah, you dae haircuts as well?" the old man said, surprised.

"Naw, naw. A Garibaldi is a biscuit," Sadie explained.

Mr Nagazumi laughed loudly. "Oh! I beg honourable pardon," he said.

Sadie thought it was about time to attack. Clearing her throat, she said, "Look, Mr Nagazumi, would ye no' please consider takin' Erchie back. He's no' bad man and we've maybe got a weddin' comin' up nd ye know how expensive weddin's can be these days."

"Honourable daughter?" Nagazumi asked.

"Aye, oor Bunty. How could Ah face masel' if Ah couldnae gie ma ain daughter a decent weddin'?"

"You a very fine lady, Mrs Hunter," Nagazumi said. "Your husband no' deseve a fine wee wumman like you."

"Ah'm beggin' ye, Mr Nagazumi. Ur ye a faither yersel'?" Sadie said in her best pleading voice.

"Have six beautiful daughters all married in marquee." Nagazumi smiled proudly.

"Ah've never been tae a weddin' in a tent," Sadie said.

"If your husband had chinged his ways, I might have taken him back for your sake," Nagazumi said.

"Oh, but he *has* chinged, Mr Nagazumi, he *has* chinged," Sadie said, seeing a glimmer of hope.

"Unfortunately we have nae vacancies for midgets," Nagazumi said.

"Could ye no' stretch a point?" Sadie asked.

"Could you no' stretch yer man?" Nagazumi replied.

"Erchie *is* a new man, Mr Nagazumi," Sadie said. "Only this mornin' he said he was gonny turn ower a new leaf and *never* con anybody ever again – *never!*" Sadie clasped her hands together in prayerful fashion..

A sudden noise from outside the door made Sadie jump. Muffled voices could be heard from the lobby and Sadie looked expectantly at her husband's former employer.

"That'll be Erchie noo," she said, relieved. "Is that you, Erchie?" she called.

"Aye, it's me," came the reply from the other side of the door.

"Mr Nagazumi's here," Sadie called.

"Auld Bloated Bags?" came the reply, "Good. Ah'll be there in a minute."

"There ye ur, then, that wisnae long for tae wait, wisit?" Sadie said.

"No, Ah have enjoyed sitting here having a conversation wi' priceless wumman who never opens her mouth."

"She's no' real, Mr Nagazumi," Sadie said, "She's made o' paper by the auld man next door. He's an origami freak."

"Ah, my auld eyes are not what they used to be!" Nagazumi groaned.

"Whit did they used tae be – jorries?" Sadie said.

The door suddenly flew open and Tyrone entered. "Hello Sadie," he cried.

"Where hiv youse been?" Sadie demanded.

"We wur at the Pavilion Theatre, so we wur," Tyrone said.

"Aye, well youse hiv nae right for tae be galavantin' roon' toon. Erchie knew Mr Nagazumi was comin' up. So, where is he?"

"Here Ah am," a voice said as a midget walked in. Nagazumi jumped up, eyes staring.

"Honourable eyes do not believe this," he gasped." He pulled himself up from the chair, bowed to Marilyn and Sadie.

Turning at the door, he said, "I shall return."

"Mr Nagazumi – come back – come back." Sadie called. But the old man was already stepping into his chauffeured Rolls Royce and was speeding away.

"Right," she said, hands on hips, "who's the Tooth Fairy here?"

Erchie stepped in grinning from ear-to-ear. "It worked didn't it?" he beamed.

66

"You're no gonny con a man like Mr Nagazumi wi' a stupit ploy like that," Sadie said angrily.

"That remains tae be seen," Erchie said.

"Ah thought Ah played ma part well," the midget piped up.

"You shut yer face and get back tae yer mushroom," Sadie snapped. The midget looked up at Erchie who nodded towards the door.

"Aye, away ye go, Rupert, Ah'll fix up wi' ye the morra."

Rupert shrugged and left.

"Right, where did ye dig him up?" Sadie asked sternly.

"Rupert?" Erchie said innocently, "He's wan o' the seven dwarfs in *Snow White* at the Pavilion. Dae ye think auld Nagazumi was fooled?"

"He might've been if that wee toad had chinged oot o' his pokey-hat costume. Who was he – Dopey?"

"Ah telt ye he should've chinged intae a suit efter the matinee," Tyrone said.

"And another thing," Sadie said, "He disnae look wan bit like you. For a start his eyebrows meet in the middle," Sadie said.

"Ma eyebrows meet in the middle," Erchie protested.

"No' in the middle o' yer chin, they don't," Sadie snapped.

"Anywey, faces don't matter," Erchie said authoritatively, "We a' look the same tae they Japs."

"Sadie wisnae fooled either, wur ye Sadie?" Tyrone said.

"That Rupert wis Erchie, ye mean?" Sadie said, raising her brows. Tyrone nodded. "Naw, Ah knew right away that that wee man wisnae Erchie. He looked too intelligent."

"Sadie's perceptive that wey," Erchie said.

"Is that yer lawsuit up in the air noo?" Sadie asked hopefully.

"Not a bit of it," Erchie said. "Ah am jist startin'."

"When Mr Nagazumi staun's up in court and tells them how ye tried tae con him wi' a midget you wull be the laughin' stock, so ye wull," Sadie said.

"Aye, well Ah thought wi' auld Nagazumi's shoart-sightedness, Ah might get away wi' it. How did he get on wi' that warrior?"

"He thought he was the windae cleaner," Sadie said, "although he began tae get suspicious when he saw he was cleanin' the same wan pane a' the time."

"Aye, well, wee Rupert lets us down," Erchie said.

"It was yer ain fault," Sadie said. "Ye should've made sure he wore a normal suit o' claeths before he came up here. Ah mean, yella and silver troosers an jaicket wi' a golden Noddy hat wi' tinkle bell on tap isnae whit ye would call normal steppin' oot apparel, is it?"

Erchie hung his head.

"Ye'll need tae get these daft ideas oot yer heid, Erchie," Sadie went on. "There's nae place for racism in this world. We ur a' Jock Tamson's bairns."

"Ah jist get angry, so Ah dae," Erchie said bitterly. "*We* won the war but they're takin' ower by the back door. They're takin' ower everthin' – even oor names. Sony, for instance. Noo, ye'd think that's a good Japanese name, Sony. But it's no'. It's frae that great Al Jolson song, *Sony Boy*, Then there's Akai – ye think that's a Japanese name, eh? Never. It's a good Scots name. Ye've heard that great Scots phrase *Akai the noo*."

"Ah never thought on that, Erchie, you're a genius so ye ur," Tyrone said in admiration.

"You shut up ya wee idiot," Erchie said.

"Ye'll be sayin' *sukiyaki*'s a good Scots word, next."

"Naw, Ah'll gie them that. Although we a' know a' aboot sookyin in an' that."

"Ah know another good Scots word they hiv stolen," Tyrone said.

"Whit's that, then?" Erchie asked.

"River Kwai," Tyrone said, pleased with himself.

"How dae ye make that oot tae be a Scots word, then?" Erchie asked.

"*River* —— efter oor River Clyde," Tyrone said.

"Another word oot o' you and Ah'll take ye doon there an' chuck ye in it," Erchie said. "But," he added, "ye're wee mind's workin' in the right direction, Tyrone."

The wee man was exalted by this accolade from Erchie. He pushed on. "Another good Scots word stolen is *Mazda*."

"How dae ye make that oot, Tyrone?" Sadie asked.

"Can ye no' see, Sadie?" Tyrone was annoyed that Sadie did not see this blatant piracy of Scot words, "*Mazda*," he repeated.

"Whit does it mean?" Sadie said.

"Mazda – it means yer gran'faither – yer Ma's Da', get it?"

"Ah'd never hiv thought aboot it," Sadie said.

"Ah'll need tae keep ma eye oan you," Erchie said, "Ye're beginnin' tae use whit wee brain ye've got, Tyrone, and that's dangerous. But Ah am right. Who *did* win the war, eh? The German's ur at the same gemme – word pinchin'. Did ye ever see *The Longest Day* Ty?"

"That's the day before Ah get ma Giro," Tyrone said.

"Naw, it's a' aboot D Day, John Wayne an' that. Ah couldnae wait tae see the end o' the film for tae see if we won or no."

"An' did we?" Tyrone asked.

"That's ma point an' that's whit Ah'm beginnin' tae wonder." Erchie said. "They'll no' hauf dae their nuts when they see their precious antique is missin', oh boy!" Erchie was beside himself.

"Whit's an antique, Erchie?" Tyrone asked.

"It's somethin' very auld an' ugly, Tyrone, jist like your faither," Erchie said.

"Is that whit him oot the windae is, an antique?" Tyrone asked.

"That's right," Erchie said.

"He's dead auld right enough," Tyrone said, " but Ah don't think they'll miss him too much. They'll jist make another wan. Ah mean they a' look the same – jist like in real life," Tyrone said.

"Naw, naw," Erchie blurted in frustration, "Ye canny jist make another wan. These things ur priceless. They're wan offs."

"Ur they a' deid?" Tyrone asked.

"He and his cronies definitely ur. They ur from a bygone age, Tyrone."

"Ah canny help feelin' sorry for him," Tyrone said, nodding towards the window. "Ah mean, look at him. Wance a brave warrior, gets killed in battle and ends up a windae cleaner."

"That's life, Tyrone," Erchie said. "Anywey, he'll be quite happy. He'll be in Heaven noo."

"Dae ye think there *is* a Heaven, Erchie?" Tyrone asked.

"There is, but don't ask me where it is," Erchie said.

"There's a Hell tae," Sadie said, "Ah can tell ye where *that* is." Tyrone went to the window.

"Och, look at him, it's pitiful. An' look, wan o' his fingers is missin'."

"Och he'll no' be worried aboot that,"Erchie said. "In Heaven everythin' is balanced oot, He'll hiv a new finger, Ah'm tellin' ye."

"Ye think so?" Tyrone asked, a happy gleam in his eye.

"Definitely," Erchie said.

"How can ye be so sure?" Tyrone asked, seriously.

"Well," Erchie began, "Ma pal, Wee Sammy McNab died suddenly wan day. Noo, Sammy had a widden leg and a good leg. We had made a pact that whoever died first would come back and tell the other wan how things was goin'. Well, Ah went alang and saw a medium . . ."

"A medium whit?" Tyrone interrupted.

"That's whit ye call people that are friendly wi' the spirits."

"Others ye call drunks," Sadie said.

Erchie ignored his wife's comments and continued with his narrative. "Well, we a' sat roon' a table an' held hauns an' the medium said 'Ur ye there, Sammy?' And, the next things wis Sammy's voice, loud an' clear came wafting ower the airwaves. 'Ah am here,' he said in an eerie voice," Erchie said, mimicking the ghostly sound.

" 'Is it true,' Ah said, 'that everything is balanced oot on the other side?' 'Aye,' he said 'No longer hiv Ah got wan good leg and wan widden leg. Ah've noo got *two* widden legs.' See whit Ah mean, Tyrone? Everythin' is set right, everythin is balanced up." Erchie wiped his brow.

"That's amazin', so it is," Tyrone said. "So, *he* wull get a new finger – even if it's jist a widden wan, that it?"

"Dead right," Erchie said. "So, y'see, they canny jist make a new wan o him. *He* was real flesh an' blood at wan time. He might've jist been an artifact in them galleries but he comes frae another eon."

"Is that the doorman's name?" Tyrone asked.

"Whit doorman?" Erchie asked

"The doorman at the Art Galleries is that his name – Eon?"

"Whit the hell ur ye talkin' aboot?" Erchie cried,"How the hell should Ah know whit the doorman's name is?"

"You said Ian – *I-A-N*," Tyrone argued.

"It's eon — *E-O-N* – it means another age, another era. Ye know whit *era* means, don't ye?

"Of coorse Ah dae," Tyrone said, hurt. "It's a good Glesca word, like ye're walkin' alang the road an' the bloke in front ye says, 'Oh, look *era* big hole in the grun'. Ah am no' daft Erchie,

An' that doorman must've been hauf blin' for tae let us walk in and walk oot with Kareoke Wullie there right under his nose."

"Well, it jist proves that when ye're right, ye're right," Erchie said. "Ah'm tellin' ye Tyrone, the finger of God is oan me."

"Which wan?" Tyrone asked.

"There is only wan God, Tyrone," Erchie said.

"Naw, Ah meant which finger?" Tyrone said

"How the hell dae Ah know which finger? It's a term – a turn of phrase," Erchie said, agitated.

"Well, personally, Ah don't think that Mr Naganooky wull gie two hoots aboot that hoarseman. They've got millions o' them. Ah saw it oan telly. They found a whole army o' they warriors, a' staunin' tae attention wi' some oan hoarses. A whole army o' them. Wan missin's no' gonny make any difference," Tyrone was pleased with himself again.

"You ur talkin' aboot the terracottas," Erchie snapped.

"Ah'm Ah?" Tyrone said, surprised. "Imagine that, me talkin' aboot them."

"They wur statues that were found," Erchie said, "And they wur *nut* Japanese – they wur Chinese. There is a big difference. This man here is a Samurai Warrior."

"Ah canny tell the difference," Tyrone said. "Ah mean *he* jist looks like the wee bloke doon in that Chinese Takeaway Wee Angus."

"Naw, they ur completely different, Tyrone jist like us an' folk frae Edinburgh. They've got completely different cultures. The Chinese gave us dynamite for instance. An' noodles. They even gave us Glesca folk the name o' their beloved country for to use in oor everyday language. The Japs never did that." Erchie stopped for breath.

"Whit word was that, Erchie?" Tyrone was all ears.

"Well, for instance, if Ah'm walkin' doon the street and Ah see you oan the other side. Whit dae Ah shout tae you?"

Tyrone thought for a moment and, after a pause, his eyes brightened. "Ah know," he said, "You'd shout: 'len' me a couple o' quid'."

"Naw, Ah widnae," Erchie groaned. "Ah'd shout: 'Hullorerr, *China* – see whit Ah mean. Ah mean, Ah widna shout, 'Hullorerr Jap, would Ah?"

"Aw. Ah see whit ye mean, Erchie," Tyrone said, dawn shining in his eyes.

"This conversation is trite," Sadie said. "We ur staunin' here wi' you, Erchie, wi' nae joab. Oor daughter might be plannin' a weddin', youse hiv robbed the Glesca Art Galleries an' we hiv a Japanese windae cleaner hingin' oot the windae. An' youse ur talkin aboot 'Hullorerr China'."

Sadie shook her head in despair just as a loud yell came from next door Tyrone jumped.

"It's ma faither," he cried. "Ah'd better ge in and see whit he waants."

"Naw, you stey here, Tyrone, Ah'll go in. Ah don't want you comin back in here. Ye might bring the whole Royal Family wi' ye. Mrs Thatcher an' Marilyn Monroe hiv been enough for wan day."

"He'll be wantin' his dummy, Sadie," Tyrone said.

"Is he no' a bit auld for a dummy?" Erchie said, surprised.

"It gies him great comfort," Tyrone said.

"Where is it? Oan his bedside table?" Sadie asked, heading for the door.

"Naw, it's in the cupboard," Tyrone said, "Ye canny miss it. It's inflated and is five-foot-six wi' blonde hair."

"Dirty auld midden," Sadie murmured as she hurried across the landing.

Suddenly the door flew open and Bunty came storming in dabbing her eyes.

"Whit's wrang, hen?" Erchie asked worriedly.

"Ah had a fight wi' Adolph," Bunty said through tears.

"Whit's wrang?" Sadie said, entering and taking in the scene with her distraught daughter.

"Aw, mammy, Adolph said ma da' was a racist," Bunty wailed.

Sadie rested Bunty's head on her shoulder and patted her affectionately. "There there, hen," she comforted. "Adolph is dead right. Don't be angry wi' 'im."

Erchie exploded. "Whit dae ye mean 'Adolph is dead right'," he mimicked Sadie's voice.

"Why don't ye admit it?" Sadie snapped.

"It's right enough, Erchie," Tyrone said, "Ye'll no' eat black puddin'."

"You shut yer face ya wee idot or Ah'll gie you a black eye."

"Is yer romance wi' Adolph ower, hen?" Sadie softly asked.

"Ah'm meetin' him the morra tae discuss oor situation," Bunty said, dabbing her eyes with a hankie.

"Don't turn up, hen," Erchie said. "Ah canny hiv a son-in-law called Adolph, Ah jist canny so Ah canny." Erchie almost wept.

"How no'?" Sadie said, "you wur goin' wi' a lassie called Molly when Ah first met ye."

"That is a good British name – nae German connotations there, so ther's no'." Erchie was adamant.

"Whit? Molly Shiklegruber?" Sadie rubbed it in.

"It was Molly *Mac*Shiklegruber – there's a difference," Erchie corrected.

"Ach away an' bile yer heid," Sadie said.

Bunty spotted the Samurai Warrior's legs dangling inside the house. She strolled over to the window and was startled.

"Oooh! Where did Genghis Khan come frae?" she gasped.

"That's no' the great English cricket captain, Genghis Khan, Bunty. That's a Summertime Warrior frae Japan," Tyrone said. "He's usually sittin' oan a joarse. But tryin' for tae get the hoarse oot the windae would've been difficult."

"So, whit's he daein' here, then?" Bunty asked, curiously.

"Er – we're jist keepin' him for somebody," Sadie volunteered.

"Dae ye think he looks a bit like ma da'?" Bunty asked, turning her head and examining the Samurai from all angles.

"Only the widden heid part," Sadie said.

"Hey come aff it," Erchie protested. "Whit makes ye say Ah've got a widden heid?"

"Erchie," Sadie began, "maist men use Brylcreem or spray for their hair. No' many use Pledge."

"Ach,away ye go," Erchie said.

"Ah think that's a great idea," Tyrone said, "get a good shine an' that."

"He disnae need Pledge for tae gie him a good shine. Every Seturday night he arrives hame wi' a good shine on him," Sadie said.

"Noo, away you an' don't worry aboot anythin'. Everythin' wull turn oot fine, you'll see," Sadie said, steering Bunty towards her bedroom door.

"Thanks, Mammy," Bunty said, pecking Sadie's cheek.

"Whit's that wee rash oan yer face, hen?" Sadie said, drawing her brows together.

"Och, it's nothin'," Bunty laughed, rubbing the offending mark. "It's jist Adolph's wee Charlie Chaplin moustache."

Erchie threw up his arms and exploded. "Did ye hear that?" he cried, "Charlie Chaplin's wee moustache? Adolphe Hitler's wee moustache, ye mean – an' ye've a chek for tae say he's no' German. If he's no' a German Ah'm Pope John Paul."

"Ye don't look a bit like him, your Holiness," Tyrone said.

"That's because Ah'm no' him, ya daft wee idiot," Erchie growled.

"Ah'm gled," Tyrone said, "otherwise ye would be talkin' Polish an' Ah widnae understaun' a word you say."

"You talk English an' Ah don't understaun' a bloody word *you* say," Erchie snapped.

"Whit aboot Genghis?" Bunty said.

"Don't worry, he'll no' attack ye, hen. He's as comatose as yer faither is oan a Seturday night."

"Ah think we should retire," Sadie said.

"Ah'm too young for tae retire," Tyrone said, "Besides Ah'm no' workin'."

"Ah meant we should call it a day. It's been quite a day. You get in there and make sure yer faither's got everythin' he needs."

"Aye, a'right," Tyrone said. "Ah'll need tae make sure he's no' got his teeth in. Ah've ran oot o' Bicyle repair patches for that dummy o' his."

"Aye, good," Sadie said. "Right, noo, you," she said to Erchie, "Ah want *him* oot o' here the morra. People ur bound tae notice. There ur no' many Jap windae cleaners workin' in this area."

Erchie said nothing but humbly shuffled in Sadie's wake into the bedroom.

CHAPTER THREE

NEXT MORNING THE PAPERS WERE FULL OF THE DARING THEFT AT the Glasgow Art Galleries. Banner headlines splashed across the front pages:

THE GREAT GLASGOW ART GALLERY ROBBERY said *The Herald*
ARISING SON screamed the *Daily Record*,
NIPPON ABOOT said *The Sun*.

Sadie came hurrying into the house after collecting her milk and rolls from the corner dairy. Frantically waving the morning's *Daily Record*, she was in a panic. Erchie jumped up thinking World War Three had started.

"Whit is it? Whit is it?" he cried.

"It's a' ower the paper the whole world's lookin' for Tojo, here – *he* wull hiv tae go," she said, trying to compose hersel.

Sadie started reading telling how the Samurai Warrior was stolen from right under the eyes of security guards. A police spokesman said it was obviously the work of professional crooks, she said. Erchie stuck out his chest.

"Professional crooks?" Sadie mocked. " You and dunderheid next door – that's a laugh! 'The article was priceless', she went on, and Mr William Nagazumi, Chairman of the Shakuti Corporation, who had sponsored the exhibition, was shocked and had collapsed on hearing the news of the theft. Police are hoping that closed circuit television cameras might show how the thieves had managed to hoodwink the guards and get away.' "

Tyrone rushed in as Sadie finished the narrative. "Ah heard it oan the wireless," he yelled, "we're famous, Erchie a couple o' professionals they said."

"Don't believe a' ye read in the papers or hear on the wireless, Tyrone," Erchie said. "You're a professional idiot, that's a'."

"Listen tae this," Sadie said, continuing to peruse the paper. " 'Two men, pushing a wheelchair, were seen leaving the building and police would like to interview these men. One was about five-feet ten inches tall, wearing a tartan bunnet and dark trousers and aged between forty and sixty. The other was about four feet two inches tall, wearing a pixie hat and was aged between forty and twelve. The pixie wearer deliberately set out to taunt the police.While he had, obviously, a small head, he had a big ego. As the pair walked down Sauchiehall Street, pixie-heid, was singing loudly, "If You Knew Sushi" – this was his way of putting his thumb to his nose at the authorities, Police expect an early arrest.'"

Erchie thought deeply about the situation. He walked over and stood gazing at the window cleaner. It was not the value of the Samurai Warrior, it was the principle. He had embarrassed Shakutis. Mr Nagazumi was a gentleman and he wondered if the old man knew the indignity the workers had to put up with – but mostly in the hands of the wee Nyaff. Erchie was glad to have got back at him in particular and hoped only that the wee Nyaff would not take it out on the workers.

Mr Nagazumi's short-sightedness had failed to recognise the precious artifact and Erchie was not surprised. Anybody who thought his elephant was a dog was definitely a candidate for *Specsavers*. Although old Nagazumi did wonder why his dog lifted its food up with its tail and he wondered where it was putting it.

"Tyrone," Sadie said, "Away you in there and see tae yer faither."

"Aye, maybe Ah should. He'll be wantin' a bite," Tyrone said.

"Wull ye gie 'im his breakfast?" Sadie inquired.

"Naw, Ah'll gie him his teeth," Tyrone said without blushing.

"Talkin' aboot teeth," Sadie said, "Genghis here looks like wan o' the Bee Gees – lovely teeth!"

"Aye, ye've got tae haun' it tae the Japs. If there's somethin' tae get yer teeth inta, they'll find it. An' whit a uniform, eh, Sadie? You always liked a man in uniform, eh?"

"Ah wance nearly eloped wi' a man in uniform," Sadie said dreamily.

"Lollipop men don't count, Sadie," Erchie said snidely.

"*You* wore a uniform when Ah first met ye, "Sadie said, grimacing, "Ah should've known then that ye wur a con man."

"Whit dae ye mean a 'con man'?" Erchie snapped.

"Ah knew ye wur in the army, Erchie, and when we arranged for tae meet that night in Barraland when you turned up in yer uniform – that was ma first inklin'."

"How did ye know?" Erchie said.

"There wurnae many generals came frae Bridgeton, Erchie," Sadie said.

"Ah was tryin' tae impress ye," Erchie said, a cheeky twinkle in his eye.

"Aye, well, Bee Gees, fancy uniform or no', Ah want *him* oot this hoose," Sadie said sternly.

"No' yet, Sadie, Ah must keep him oot the road till he fills ma purpose. That wee Nyaff wull be hivin' fits right noo – he's a fanatic."

"The war's been ower mair than fifty years, Erchie. It's aboot time ye realised that. Ah'm sure him ye call the 'Wee Nyaff' has put it behind him – long forgotten. Besides, he widnae even hiv been born then."

"He was either born then or he's been seein' too many William Holden pictures."

"Well, we canny keep this yin hingin' oot the windae much longer, he'll draw attention tae himsel'," Sadie said.

"Never mind, hen, " Erchie said. "Efter this is a' ower we'll be back tae normal again – you and me – back tae happy married bliss. We've had oor ups an' downs, hen, but so has every couple. Think o' the good times – like oor first wee hoose – eh?"

"Aye," Sadie said, her mind going back, "oor wee single-end. Up in the moarnin' – a good plateful o' porridge and a cup o' tea and oot in the drivin' snaw tae work – cairryin' hunnerweights o' coal up a' they stairs. It was a different world. You wur lucky, Erchie, you went back tae bed."

"Aye, happy days! Ah used tae wonder where you got the strength frae tae hunk that coal up them stairs. But they *wur* happy days. How proud Ah wis o' oor wee Bunty. Remember she wis a flower girl at yon weddin'? You' bought her the lovely wee froack frae *Madame Oxfams*. Ah, she was a wee picture, so she wis. Ah canny remember whose weddin' it wis when she wis a flower girl." Erchie relived the past.

"It wis *Oors*, Erchie," Sadie said.

"Er – aye," Erchie said, running his finger under his collar,

"Look at her noo, eh, a young wumman who might be plannin' her ain weddin' soon – tae a Kraut," he spat out the word.

"Noo, you don't know that, Erchie, " Sadie said, coming to her daughter's defence. "He might no' be a German. Nane o' us hiv met him and Ah've only spoke tae him on the phone when he called wance and asked tae speak tae Bunty."

"Well, that should hiv gied you a clue. Did he speak wi' a German accent?" Erchie said worriedly.

"Ah couldnae tell, "Sadie said.

Tyrone entered smiling. "He's sleepin' noo," he said.

"How can ye tell?" Erchie said.

"*Erchie*," Sadie scolded.

"Noo, goin' back tae whit we wur talkin' aboot," Erchie said, "If ye spoke tae Herman or Adolph or whitever his name is on the phone. You *should* be able for tae tell by his accent frae whit part of the planet Earth does he come frae."

"Ah couldnae tell," Sadie said apologetically.

"Ah could believe that," Tyrone said, "Ah know some Germans that can talk better English than whit Ah can."

"Ah know some *parrots* that can talk better English than whit you can," Erchie sniped.

"That's no' nice, Erchie," Sadie said.

"Never mind that," Erchie said, "Tell me exactly whit Goebels said on the phone that you canny tell if he's a German or no'?"

"He only said wan phrase – 'Is Fraulein Hunter in?'" Sadie said.

Erchie threw up his arms. "Is Fraulein Hunter in?" he mimicked Sadie's voice. "*That* should've telt ye he wisnae frae Govan."

"Ach, Ah'm fed up wi' a' this nonsense. Jist you get Gunga Din there oot o' this hoose," Sadie nagged.

"Is that whit ye call him, Sadie – Gunga Din?" Tyrone was curious.

"It disnae matter whit we call him," Sadie snapped, "He's no' steyin' here."

"Who wis Gunga Din?" Tyrone asked.

"*You* ur an ignorant get, so ye ur," Erchie said. "*Everybody* knows who Gunga Din wis."

"Ah don't," Tyrone said.

"You don't even know who *you* ur," Erchie said. "Gunga Din was a great hero frae literature," Erchie began to explain.

"Is that near Liverpool?" Tyrone asked.

"Is whit near Liverpool?" Erchie said, raising his brows.

"That place ye said Gung Din was frae – Literature or somethin'."

"Geez, whit a dumbell!" Erchie cried, "Whit school did you go tae – Saint Numbskulls? Literature is a' aboot writing – great books an' that. Gunga Din was a character in a great poem writtin by Rudyard Kipling. Gunga wis a water boy. He wis always there on the battlefield, in India, lookin' efter the British sojers. He wis always ready for that painful cry and always had a skinful – jist like your faither. The dyin' sojer might be lyin' there under the blazin' sun gaspin' for a drink. 'Gunga', would be his painful cry and Gunga was by his side wi' a big drink o' watter. First he would gie him a drink, then brush his teeth wi' a nylon toothbrush, gie him a shave, usin a brush made of the very finest camel hair. Then he would get the man to his feet and brush him doon, usin' the very latest in goats' hair brushes . Then he would spit on the man's shoes and poalish them wi' a brush made frae the hair of a llama. He became famous a' because of a British colonel. It was a fierce battle and the colonel was lyin' oan the grun wi' umteen spears stuck in him – but he winae deid. He wis jist thirsty. 'Gunga' he shouted and Gunga raced tae his side. First he took the auld colonel's teeth oot and brushed them wi' his super nylon toothbrush. Then he pressed the auld colonel's troosers wi' him still in them. Gunga had wan o' they new 'Press yer troosers while ye ur still weerin' them' irons. Then he did a' the other things Ah telt ye aboot. The colonel was that grateful he took Gunga's haun and pressed it affectionately an' said those immortal words. '*You're a better betterwear man than I am, Gunga Din*'."

"Did the auld colonel die?" Tyrone asked, dabbing his eyes.

"He had eighteen spears stickin' in him, Tyrone," Erchie said. "He was a very religious man so he would be pleased for tae hiv have a holey death, eh?"

"Whit happened tae Gunga?" Tyrone asked.

"He became a big noise in literature – hence the word *Din*. If they hidnae said that, you'd be callin' a great racket a Gunga."

79

"Aye, well, there' gonny be a great Gunga in this hoose in a minute if Tojo there isnae got rid of," Sadie said.

"A'right, a'right," Erchie said with impatience. "Come on, Tyrone, gie's a haun'."

The two men manhandled the warrior out of the window and into the house.

"Whit dae we dae wi' him noo, then?" Erchie said.

"Ah don't care whit ye dae wi' him, jist get him oot o' here," Sadie said.

"Ah'll hiv tae chew this owr in ma mind," Erchie said. Then he put the sittingSamurai on a chair facing Marilyn Monroe.

"Whit if somebody comes in an' sees him?" Sadie said.

"Ah'll jist say its ma prop for ma karaoke debut," Tyrone said.

"Whit dae ye mean?" Sadie said.

"Well, whit better prop for a karaoke than somethin' for per-tainin' to that country where the karaoke was born.? Look – " Tyrone lifted the Warrior and sat down on the chair, placing him on his knee. Then gritting teeth said. "A Gottle of geer – a Gottle of geer." He could not get the head to turn but reckoned he could give a good account of himself in the ventriloquist stakes.

"That's nae good," Erchie said. "No' only could Ah see your mooth movin', Ah could see *his* mooth wis movin'."

"How is that possible?" Tyrone said. "*He* is an inaminate object."

"That make two o' ye," Erchie said.

"Cover him up," Sadie commanded.

"Ah hiv tae think whit tae dae wi' him," Erchie said. "Here, sit him in the cludge tae Ah decide. "Right, Tyrone c'mon."

"Bathroom, Erchie, the word is *bathroom*, nut cludge." Sadie snapped.

They struggled with the sitting figure and managed to get him in the proper position in the toilet.

"Hey, Sadie, "Tyrone said, "your bathroom looks jist like oor cludge."

"Shut yer face ya ignorant wee swine," Erchie said. "Noo, leave him sittin' there until ma mind clears. How aboot a cuppa coffee, hen?" he added.

Sadie put on the kettle and the dynamic duo sat down at the table. Erchie switched on the television. Angus Simpson had just started to read the early news on Scottish Television.

"Police have released video of the two men suspected of stealing the Samurai Warrior from the Glasgow Art Galleries," he began. Pictures flashed up on the screen of Erchie and Tyrone hurrying away from the building pushing a wheelchair.

"Police would like anyone who saw the pair, whose faces are hidden by black bin bags, to come forward. A substantial reward has been offered by Mr William Nagazumi, Chairman of the Shakuti Corporation which sponsored the exhibition.

"It's been reported that Mr Nagazumi has been ordered to the Japanese Embassy, in London, where, it is assumed, his fingernails will be pulled off and his two-inch long hair will have a three-inch long haircut."

"That's terrible!"Sadie said, "such a nice man tae. An' see that black bin bag ye wore ower yer head?"

"Aye, whit aboot it?* Erchie said.

"Would ye consider wearin' it a' the time?"

"Aw, very funny," Erchie said.

⋆　⋆　⋆

The days passed and the robbery slid down the newsworthy schedules. Mr Nagazumi, it was reported, had been to London and had now returned wearing knitted steel wool oven gloves. The effect of his derring do was not what Erchie had expected. It was reported that Mrs Thatcher was delighted with her effigy and was riding into Glasgow in a kimono to plug her book, "Samurai Waitin' in the Wings". When a reporter asked how she liked her paper cut-out she is reported to have said, "Shut yer face ya skelly wee midden".

Sadie was angry that Tojo had not been ejected from the Hunter household. "Look, Erchie," she said, "Ah'm fed up goin' in for a bath and that grinnin' wee Nyaff sittin' here watchin' me. Ur you sure he's no real?"

"If he was real he'd fly oot that door in a flash," Erchie said.

Strathclyde police had every available man on the job. The Mrs Thatcher cut-out was sent to the Forensic department at Glasgow University who immediately confirmed it was made out of old newspapers. They seemed no nearer to finding the missing artifact or the culprits who had taken it. And Sadie was getting more uncomfortable. Filling in her lottery that week she marked down the numbers one-eight-two two-one-six. Erchie queried this as they always put down birthdays and addresses but Sadie explained that these were special numbers – 182-216 – her high blood pressure count.

Sadie's nagging was getting to Erchie and he reluctantly agreed to move the Warrior out of the bathroom. With Tyrone's help he manhandled the Samurai out of the bathroom and into the living room.

"Right, whit dae we dae wi' him noo?" Erchie said, wiping his brow.

"Intae the bedroom," Tyrone said.

"Naw, naw," Sadie said. "The bathroom wis bad enough. But he is *nut* goin' intae the bedroom – no' that anythin' happens in there except sleep. But Ah couldnae thole him sittin' there at ma bedside, his teeth glintin' like a row o' tombstones."

"Right, oot the windae again – get the shammy," Erchie said. Once more the Samurai was placed outside the window, legs dangling in and with chamois in hand. No sooner had the warrior been placed when there was a loud knock at the door. Sadie jumped two feet in the air.

"Who could that be?" she gasped, "It canny be Tyrone's faither, he'll still be in bed wi' his dummy."

"Ah'll get it," Erchie said bravely.

Mr Nagazumi raised his bowler hat and bowed.

"Ah, Mrs Hunter," he said, "You lookin' well. How is honourable man, Erchie? He still shrinking or you now calling him Tommy after Honourable Tommy Thumb, eh?"

Nagazumi laughed loudly at his own joke. Erchie said nothing but showed him in and steered him towards a chair. Tyrone had gone to stand in front of the window with his arms outstretched.

Nagazumi spotted Tyrone, who was trying to block the window. "Is honorable wee man on some religious kick?" he said.

"Oh, that's oor next door neighbour," Sadie said, "he thinks he's an aeroplane."

"Watch he don't fly oot window – he might knock honourable windae cleaner off."

"Aye, well, Erchie used tae dae the windaes himsel'," Sadie said, " but he's frightened he might get swooped doon on and flown oaff in th beak o' a hungry seagull."

"He *should* definitely be picked up by the beak – or should I say 'sent doon' by the beak," Mr Nagazumi said.

"Whit does he mean, Erchie?" Tyrone said, breaking his silence.

"He means Ah should be up in court an' sent tae jail, Tyrone," Erchie said.

"Ah, honourable Erchie is back to normal, eh?" said the not-so-dumb Mr Nagazumi.

"Er – well – er – aye," Erchie stammered. "As ye can clearly see. Ah've taken a stretch."

"You should go away for a stretch," Nagazumi said.

"Aye, well – er, we a' make mistakes," Erchie said.

"Your honourable maw made wan big wan," Nagazumi said.

"Ah'm awfu' sorry for tae hear aboot yer trouble at the art gallery, Mr Nagazumi," Sadie said.

"Aye, well, there will be good reward for finder of honourable Samurai," the old man said.

"How is yer haun's," Erchie asked, "Ah heard ye wur tae get yer nails puulled oot."

"That not true. New steel wool oven gloves presented to me by honourable ambassador for very special reason."

"Whit was that?" Erchie asked.

"So I no' burn honourable haun' openin' oven door," Nagazumi said.

"Ye mean they didnae threaten ye wi' violence because ye allowed the Samurai for tae be stolen?" Erchie said in disbelief.

"Oh yes," Nagazumi said with a wry smile. "They threatened to make me honourable contestant in Japanese competitive show."

"That's the shows where ye've tae climb mountains in yer bare feet an', when ye get tae the tap, jump intae the mooth o' a volcano an' that," Tyrone said.

"Ah dae that every time Ah come hame wi' a broken pey," Erchie said.

"You got honorable lovely wife," Nagazumi said. "You got any weans?"

"Oh, aye, we've got a daughter, Bunty," Erchie said proudly. "And she might be gettin' married soon tae a German called Herr somethin'."

"Herr cut?" Nagazumi laughed.

Tyrone joined in his laughter with loud guffaws.

"Aw, that wis funny, Mr Naggyzumi," he said.

"You shut yer wee face," Erchie snapped.

"Me got a dog," Nagazumi said.

"Ah've never had the pleasure o' meetin' yer wife," Erchie said.

"Honourable wee dog is a German Shepherd," Nagazumi said proudly.

"They're no' as nice as alatians," Tyrone said.

"Shut yer geggie, you," Erchie said. "Tell me, Mr Nagazumi, you hiv had an interestin' life. Ur ye plannin' for to write yer memories?"

Mr Nagazumi held up his hands. "Have very sore hands and am getting shiatzu every Friday," he said.

"Ah'll bet that first started wi' ye when yer sojer got nicked," Erchie said smugly.

"No, started getting it in Japan. You no' get it here on National Health?"

"Only when Ah see the price o' the prescriptions," Erchie said.

"Whit is it ye get again, Mr Nagazumi?" Tyrone inquired.

"Shiatzu," he replied – "every Friday."

"Erchie gets that every Seturday efter a vindaloo usually," Sadie said.

"Oh, you have other illnesses besides shrink-itis?" Nagazumi said, turning to Erchie.

"Ah've got it, tae," Tyrone said, "But we call it constipation."

"No, no – no' constipation," Nagazumi said. "Shiatzu is name of Japanese therapy. Honourable therapist puts fingers on sore parts of body and relieves pain."

"Sadie puts her fingers in ma poackets an relives me of ma money," Erchie said.

Sadie glowered at her husband.

"You say nothing bad about honourable wife," Nagazumi rebuked. "She very nice person. Reminds me of my own loved one."

"Yer wife?" Erchie said.

"My dear parent."

"Yer maw?" Erchie asked.

"Ma da'," Nagazumi said in his best Glasgow accent.

Ngazumi took Sadie's hand in his and bowing, kissed it.

"Excuse ma haun's, Mr Nagazumi," Sadie said. "They're never oot the sink. D'ye think they're a bit rough?"

"Naw, naw," Nagazumi said, "but could offer you job in factory as honourable paint stripper."

"Here, ur you suggestin' that ma wife's haun's ur rough?" Erchie said angrily.

"State of honourable Sadie's hands have nothing to do with her beautiful disposition," Nagazumi said.

"Ma Sadie's lovely haun's are as delicate as tissue paper," Erchie said.

"Emery paper," Nagazumi corrected.

"Oh, ye're a real wag, Mr Nagazumi," Sadie twittered.

"That not nice thing to say to honourable me," Nagazumi said.

"Ah said ye wur a wag – that's a man that's funny," Sadie said.

"Beg honourable pardon," Nagazumi said, "Ah thought you said Ah was a wog."

"Look, it's very warm in here," Tyrone said, "Ah'll open the windae a bit, eh? Jist a chink, if ye'll pardon the expression, Mr Nagazumi."

Nagazumi rose and strolled over to the window, "Window cleaner still on same pane as last time," he said.

"Er – Mr Nagazumi," Sadie said, "Whit did ye come up here for?"

"I wanted to see shrinking man but can see he has grown very quickly."

"Ah hiv decided for to drap ma suit against ye as Ah can see that ye hiv worse troubles – yer stuff gettin' stole an' that," Erchie said.

"He's a' hert, ma Erchie," Sadie said proudly

"He's definitely no' a' heid," Nagazumi said.

"Dae ye no think he should be rewarded for drappin' his lawsuit," Sadie said.

"Only reward wull be for return or information of whereabouts of honorable Samurai," Nagazumi said.

"Ye'll no' gie him his joab back, then?" Sadie said.

"Your windae cleaner faster worker than your Erchie was," Nagazumi said.

"It was that gaffer o' yours, the wee Nyaff, who got me well an' truly riled," Erchie said.

"You turned up for work at eight o'cloack in mornin' already like that," Nagazumi said.

"Never!" Erchie said, "Never did Ah turn up for work truly well riled."

"Beg honourable pardon. Ah thought you said 'Well iled," Nagazumi said..

"Wee Nyaff is lady wife's brother so must keep him on payroll or lady wife withdraw conjugal rights," Nagazumi said sadly.

"You mean an auld man o' your age demands and gets rights frae his wife?" Sadie said.

"Yes, she good at giving me rights," Nagazumi said "– and, sometimes lefts."

Sadie and Erchie exchanged glances and smiled. But Erchie's smile vanished as Nagazumi removed his glasses, polished them with his handkerchief and peered closely at the 'window cleaner'. Then, replacing his glasses, he took a step back and looked at the figure from every angle.

"Something up, Mr Nagazumi?" Erchie asked nervously.

"For a minute I thought honourable windae cleaner resembled humble wife. But naw – too ugly."

"The windae cleaner?" Erchie asked.

"The wife," Nagazumi said.

Bunty suddenly came bursting into the room. She wept bitterly and flopped on to the easy chair.

"Whit's up, hen?" Sadie said hurrying to her daughter's side.

"It's a' ower – finished," Bunty wailed.

"Whit is?" Sadie asked, putting a comforting arm around Bunty's shoulder.

"Adolph has run away wi' a frau," she sobbed.

"Ye mean yer boyfriend's ran away wi' a wee frog?" Tyrone said with disbelief.

"*Frau*, Tyrone, *Frau*," Erchie cried, "It's a German wifie – nothin' tae dae wi' frogs.

" Ah fun' oot when Ah went for tae pick up oor costumes for the Fancy dress party the night," Bunty said, dabbing her eyes.

"Yer party's the night, hen?" Sadie said with sympathy.

"He was gonny go as his maw," Bunty said, "But the Groucho Marx moustache wis gonny be a problem."

"Has Adolph got a Groucho Marx moustache?" Sadie asked.

"Naw, his maw has ," Bunty said. "Anywey, it's a' ower."

"Efter you gettin' that lovely wig, tae," Sadie said.

"Well, hair today, gone tomorrow," Erchie said beaming. "Ah am jist gled you ur back on the market again, hen. Never mind, there ur plenty mair fish in the sea. Ye'll get another chance for tae wear yer wig."

"Ah know, da'," Bunty said, "Ah'll be wearin' it in aboot two 'oors time for the party. Ah've already hooked another fish and he'll be pickin' me up."

"Geez, that was quick," Erchie said.

"Honourable Bunty is very good looking girl," Nagazumi said, "she get fish anywhere."

"Ur ye up for to collect yer son, Mr Nagazumi?" Bunty asked.

"Son?" Nagazumi asked, raising his eyebrows.

"The windae cleaner – is that no' your son daein' a wee bit moonlightin'?"

"Him no' honourable son. Son no' do extra work. He no' even do any work.

"Jist like Erchie, here," Sadie said. Then, pleading, "Mr Nagazumi, would ye no' consider —"

Nagazumi cut her off in mid-sentence. Holding up his hand, he said, "You a good wee wumman, Mrs Erchie. Your husband no appreciate you and I am sorry for you. He no' a shrinking man and daft trying it on with me. If anybody could have got him his job back in honourable factory it was you. But have many problems on humble plate and still no convinced that dishonorable Erchie got nothing to do with theft of Samurai Warrior. It very embarrasing to me."

"Right enough," Tyrone said. "Instead o' a wee yella face you've got a red face. A' ye need is a green face and ye could be a traffic light." Tyrone laughed loudly at his weak joke.

"You shut yer face or *your* face wull be two different colours," Erchie said, "black an' blue."

Mr Nagazumi ignored Tyrone's insulting remark. Bowing he kissed Bunty' hand. "Your boyfriend no' deserve you," he said.

Then, kissing Sadie's hand, "You lovely lady. Here, take my card, and anytime I can be of any assistance to you, just contact humble servant." Turning at the door, bowed once more and said: "*Sayonara.*"

"Whit a nice man!" Bunty said.

"And yer faither had the cheek tae try and make a fool o' him," Sadie said, glowering at Erchie.

"So," Erchie said, turning to Bunty, and quickly changing the subject, "we ur gonny get the opportunity of meeting this new Adonis you've got, eh?"

"Aye, he's lovely," Bunty said, "so kind and attentive. He opens doors for me and staun's up when I walk intae the lounge bar," she said dreamily.

"How? Is he lyin' oan the flair when ye walk intae the pub?" Tyrone asked.

"Don't show yer ignorance," Erchie snapped. "It's whit a man's supposed tae dae when a wumman enters a room."

"Whit if he's deid?" Tyrone asked,

"Then he canny staun' up, can he?" Erchie said despairingly.

"Only if he's Dracula," Tyrone said.

"Aw, shut yer face – Dracula – whit rubbish," Erchie shook his head.

"Aye, well, Ah'm away ben and get prepared for ma date," Bunty said, and hurried off.

"And Ah'm away intae the clu – er – bathroom for a shave," Erchie said. leaving Sadie, Tyrone and Marilyn Monroe alone.

Sadie sighed. "Aw, stick her oot the road – in the cupboard, there."

Tyrone gently lifted 'Marilyn' and placed her in the broom cupboard.

"Ah don't think it's right that ma da's lovely Marilyn should be stuck in a cupboard wi' a' the brushes. It's no' like she was a scrubber or somethin'," Tyrone protested.

"Aye, ye're right," Sadie said. "That lassie had enough troubles hersel'. Take her back intae yer faither."

Tyrone retrieved Marilyn and stopped at the door as Sadie called out "Don't be comin' back wi' anybody else noo."

Tyrone agreed. and was back in a flash – empty handed.

"Oh, look!" Sadie called. "Mr Nagazumi has forgot his bowler hat. Run doon and see if ye can catch him, Ty."

But Tyrone had just opened the door when a breathless Mr Nagazumi walked in.

"Forget to lift bowley hat," he gasped, "It is badge of humble authority."

"Mr Nagazumi, "Sadie said, about to hand over the hat, "Ah am embarrassed by a' this."

"I say again," Nagazumi said, "you very nice lady and you stand by your man as as Tammy Winedrap sings. That is loyalty and if dishonourable Erchie had some o' it he might still be in good Shakutis joab."

He took his hat and turned to go.

"Please Mr Nagazumi," Sadie said taking hold of his elbow, "for me, please. Would ye no' consider hivin' him back? Ah know he is still fightin' the war but he's no' really a bad man."

"That is problem in this world," Nagazumi said, " there is no forgiveness."

"Erchie is a racist or so he thinks," Sadie said.

"He'll no' eat black puddin'," Tyrone added.

"Quiet, Tyrone," Sadie snapped.

"But he loves curries," Tyrone added as a softener.

Erchie entered from the bathroom drying his hands.

"Ye're still here, Mr Nagazumi?" he said.

"Talking to lovely wife, Mrs Sadie. You should be very proud of her," Nagazumi said.

"Whit make ye think Ah'm no'?" Erchie said.

"Look at claeths she wears, that tells me," Nagazumi said.

"Ah get ma claeths in the *Reject Shoap*," Sadie said. "That's where Ah got Erchie."

Nagazumi laughed.

"That is nut true," Erchie protested. "Ah arranged for you tae hiv a credit card."

"For the *Oxfam* shoap," Sadie sniped.

"Ah'll get ye a mair up-market credit cerd, hen," Erchie said.

"*Sue Ryder* disnae issue credit cards," Sadie said.

"Ah could believe all you say, dear wee wumman," Nagazumi said. "You got a drone of a man. He no' even speak good language in factory."

"He only knows bad language," Sadie said.

"He no' even speak the language his employers speak very bad, that," Nagazumi said.

"Ah canny speak Japanese," Erchie cried.

"I meant English," Nagazumi said. "However, must go, try and find honourable twelfth-century Samurai Warrior."

Nagazumi bowed, raised his hat and left.

"That's a diabolical shame!" Sadie said. "Treatin' that nice auld man like that."

"Ah canny abandon ma principles," Erchie said.

"You hivnae got any principles," Sadie said. "Ye're still fightin' the war and ye even had yer daughter greetin' because ye didnae approve o' her boyfriend, a boy ye hadnae even met."

"He was a German, wint he? That's a' Ah need tae know," Erchie snapped.

"But ye didnae know, that's the point," Sadie said. "Ye jumped on her when ye heard whit his name was."

"You ur not politically correct, Erchie, "Tyrone said with courage.

"You shut yer trap," Erchie commanded.

An authoritative knock on the door made them jump.

"Och, who is it this time?" Erchie moaned.

"It maybe Bunty's new boyfreen'. Ah'll get it," she said opening the door.

CHAPTER FOUR

SADIE ANSWERED THE DOOR TO A SMALLISH MAN WEARING A homburg hat. Without an invitation and with an air of authority he walked into the room. His narrow eyes swept the room and he cleared his throat.

"Ah am Detective Inspector Hamish McSponger, NYPD," he said in a low growl.

"NYPD?" Erchie asked, raising his brows.

"New Yorkhill Proddy Division," the policeman said, "sometimes known as NYPD – Blue noses, that is."

Erchie and Sadie glanced at each other.

"Ah've seen youse on the telly," Tyrone said.

"Shut yer face, eejit," Erchie said. "A' you watch oan the telly is The Tellytubbies. Whit can Ah dae for you, Inspector?"

McSponger stuck a cigar in his mouth and began to chew on it. "Ah am lookin' for a Samurai Warrior," he said.

"Geez! Ur things as bad as that in New Yorkhill?" Erchie said facetiously.

"Said Samurai Warrior is from the land of Japan and we only hud a lenny it for to show in oor esteemed art galleries. But two villians hiv secreted it away – whit aboot you?" he turned to Tyrone.

"Ah hiv nae idea whit ye're talkin' aboot," Tyrone said, through shaking knees.

"How's that?" the inspector asked.

"'Cos he disnae know whit anybody's talkin' aboot," Erchie said.

"You'd better speak up if ye know whit's good for ye," the inspector said. "This is a very serious felony, y'know."

"Well, Ah hiv never been serious in ma life and this is a felony-body knows and it's no' me."

"This Warrior was astride a hoarse and he was replaced by a very important person."

"Ah do nut know or hiv conversations wi' any very important

91

persons," Tyrone said haughtily.

"He disnae even know any *un*important persons," Erchie said unkindly.

"Well, it has come tae ma notice that this Warrior was transported in a wheelchair and you, wee man, was seen shovin' a wheelchair, so ye wur."

"That was ma faither in that wheelchair," Tyrone said.

"Well wee man, your faither is the spittin' image of Mrs Thatcher," McSponger said. He strolled around the room, watched closely by Erchie and Sadie ever hoping that he would not go near the window. He opened the top drawer of the oak sideboard.

"Ye'll no' find him in there that's for sure," Sadie said.

"Oh, Ah don't know," Mc Sponger said. "A wee bird telt me a' sorts o' strange tales aboot this hoose."

"Like whit for instance?" Sadie said, her hump rising.

"Like incredible shrinkin' men, for instance," McSponger said.

"Ye don't believe a' ye hear," Sadie said.

"Ah am cognizent of the fact that wan, Erchie Hunter, has been sacked from Shakutis, the great Japanese factory, that had arranged the priceless exhibition. Ah hiv spoke to the Chairman, a Mr Sukiyaki, or somethin', who feels that wan Erchie Hunter, might hiv taken umbrage at bein' fired and decided for tae gie him a red face."

"Ah hiv never taken umbrage in ma life, hiv Ah Tyrone?" Erchie protested vehemently.

"Never!" Tyrone said. "Erchie is a Guinness drinker. Ah am sure he has never even ever tasted umbrage, so he hisnae."

"A Classroom o' schoolweans wur present in the gallery when this terrible felony was perpr – er – perp – er – did. Wan minute they schoolweans ur lookin' at a mighty Japanese warrior on a hoarse an' the next time they look, it's chinged intae Mrs Thatcher. That was a shock," McSponger said.

Sadie agreed saying it would have been a shock even if she weren't on a horse.

"So, whit aboot youse bein' seen pushin' this ere wheelchair, then, eh?" McSponger asked, narrowing his eyes.

"It's been a mistake," Tyrone said. "The only time that wheelchair is oot in the street is on Guy Fawkes night. Ma da' hires his wheelchair oot tae the weans for tae shove aroon their dummy in."

"Oh, aye," McSponger said suspiciously. "And whit does he dae that for?"

"Two quid," Tyrone said.

"For five quid they get his faither as well," Erchie said.

Mc Sponger paced up and down in deep thought. He stroked his chin. "Ur you sure ye did nut hiv yer faither oot yesterday and ye was shovin' him aboot in his wheelchair?" he said.

"Ma da' hisnae been oot his bed for four years. He jist lies therea' day playin' wi' his origami," Tyrone said.

"*That* is an instrument Ah've always wanted tae be able tae play. *Oh, Ah Do Like To Be Beside The Seaside,*" McSponger sang accompanied by a few dance steps.

"It took ma da' years for tae perfect it," Tyrone said. "It a' started wan day wi' a pair o' scissors and page three in the *Daily Record.* That was the beginnin' and he's never stopped."

"MM!" McSporran murmured. "That is very unusual. Maist people start wi' a comb and some tishy paper. Anywey, that's gettin' away frae the subject. Noo, somebody must've seen somethin'. Whit aboot yer windae cleaner there. A bird's eye view he's got."

"Whit windae cleaner ur ye talkin' aboot?" Sadie asked.

"Him – him hingin' oot yer windae there. That Jap fella. He might've seen somethin'."

"Naw, he widnae see anythin'," Sadie said. "He disnae speak English and is hauf blin' an' deef an' that's no' countin' his arthritis."

"And he still cleans windaes?" McSponger said in disbelief.

"Oh, aye, he's perfect," Sadie said. "He sees nuthin', hears nuthin' and canny repeat anythin'. He never talks."

"Ah don't think he washes windaes either," the policeman said, "he hisnae moved frae that wan pane since Ah came in."

"That's because he's meticulous, " Sadie said. "He'll keep at that wan pane until it's perfect. It takes him twelve years tae dae a conservatory."

"It's no' oaften ye see such a conscientious worker these days," McSponger said. Then cupping his hands to his mouth, he shouted at the 'windae cleaner', "Keep up the good work, son,

and Ah'd go and see aboot that frozen shooder if Ah was you."
Turning to Erchie, he added, "That erm hisnae budged an inch."

"Naw, he's a'right," Erchie said. "It's his tea break the noo, but
he never comes in for it. He jist goes intae wan o' they yogi
trances. He'll no' even leave the windae sill."

"Ye mean he goes intae a yogi trance even when he's sittin' oot
the windae?" McSponger was full of admiration.

"Oh, aye," Erchie said, "if he hisnae finished yer windaes he
can sleep out there for 'oors. In fact he wance turned up tae dae
oor windaes wearin' a pair o' pyjamas and a nightcap plus a hoat
watter boattle."

"Aye, it's good tae see a man who can sit oot a windae, see
whit's goin' on inside the hoose an' a'roon' aboot him and keep it
a' tae himsel." McSponger said.

"Aye, no' joke George Formby, he sang it tae a' the world,"
Sadie said.

"Aye, ye're windy cleaner is a man of high morals," the cop
said.

"Oh, ye've noticed his teeth, hiv ye?" Tyrone piped up.

"Ah never said a thing aboot his teeth, "McSponger said.

"Ah thought ye mentioned his high molars," Tyrone said.

McSponger was getting impatient. He was getting nowhere in
his investigation. He asked Tyrone if he would take him in to see
his father and Tyrone agreed. The pair left but not before
McSponger had warned Erchie and Sadie not to leave town. He
was going next door merely to eliminate Tyrone's old man from
his inquiries.

The old man lay still in bed, his mouth wide open. McSponger
stood at the foot of the bed, notebook in hand, and jotted down
something.

"Well that's ma da'," Tyrone said. "Ye can see he is bedbound."

"You did *nut* tell me that yer faither was a blonde wi' red lip-
stick oan," McSponger said.

"Naw, that's his dummy – his inflatable companion," Tyrone
said.

"Mmm! Very nice!" McSponger said. "Canny talk back either."

"Well, whit dae ye think, then?" Tyrone asked.

"Yer auld man looks like he's past it. And if ye put ony mair stickin' plasters oan that blonde she'll be past it. But Ah am nut here for to see auld men lyin' in bed wi' rubber dolls. Ah am here on the very serious business of trying to find whit happened tae a priceless Samurai Warrior which was nicked."

The two men returned next door.

"It's worth a loat o' money, is it, then?" Tyrone said.

"It is priceless but it's no' the money that matters. It's oor relations," the policeman said.

"Whit's your relations got tae dae wi' it?" Tyrone said.

"No' *ma* relations!" McSponger snapped, "It's oor country's relations wi' Japan. This priceless exhibition was entrusted tae us for to show aff to oor people. It was up tae us tae take care of it − tae look efter it. We hiv let Japan down. We hiv let Mr Nagiwhits'is name down. Ah must really solve this case. It would be good for oor prestige."

"Whit's yer double glazing got tae dae wi' it?" Tyrone asked.

"Ah don't think you ur the ful shullin', son." McSponger said. Then, turning to Erchie, he said. "Noo, listen, if anybody comes tae that door and oaffers you a Samurai Warrior jist remember it fell aff the back o' a lorry."

"Ah thought it fell aff the back o' a hoarse," Tyrone said.

McSponger ignored Tyrone and walked over to the window where he stood, hands behind his back, and knees bending, remarked. "That windae cleaner hisnae moved a muscle."

"He's great," Erchie said, "For a windae cleaner he's definitely got somethin'."

"*Rigor mortis*, Ah think," McSponger said. "Does he always hiv that grin on his face?"

"Only when he's got his teeth in," Sadie said, "and, besides, he loves his work. He's a prize!"

"Ah think ye'll need tae prise him aff that windae sill," McSponger said. "When he wakens up wull he dae another pane?"

"Oh, aye, he's thorough," Erchie said.

"Aye, well, Ah suppose Ah'd better go and continue ma search for they crooks," McSponger said.

"Tell me Inspector," Erchie said, "whit does this Japanese sojer look like?"

"Well, for a start ye widnae say he came frae Millport. He's a Japanese warrior frae a long, past dynasty," McSponger said.

"Ah used tae watch that programme," Tyrone said, "*Dynasty* wisnae as good as *High Road*, though."

"Right, then, Ah'm away," McSponger said. "Ah hiv two culprits tae catch."

Turning at the door, he said, "When he gets finished waashin' that windae would ye send him ower tae ma hoose if he's got a spare week. Ah'd like him tae clean the pane in ma dug's kennel."

McSponger left with a wave of his hand. Sadie immediately turned on Erchie.

"Right," she snapped. "Get him oot o' here," Sadie jabbed her thumb at their guest. "Yer ploy, Erchie, did nothin' except maybe gie auld Mr Nagazumi a sore heid. Ye only made a fool o' yersel' and an auld man. Ye didnae make a fool o' Tyrone 'cos he was wan tae start wi'. But it's ower an it's done nothin' for ye. So, get him oot o' here right this minute. Tell Mr Nagazumi ye've got him although Ah didnae see how Inspector Clouseau didnae recognise him. For Mr Nagazumi at least there's the excuse o' his bad eyesight." Sadie could not hide her anger.

"Ah've never seen ye as angry as this, Sadie, since that day ye caught me, knowin' yer maw liked a good gargle, pourin' a boattle o' whisky doon her throat."

"She was lyin' in her coaffin at the time," Sadie snapped.

"Well, Ah am *nut* gonny tell Nagazumi that Ah have his Samurai. Ah would lose face," Erchie said.

"That would still leave ye wi' wan," Sadie said.

"Ah'm no' daein' it," Erchie was adamant.

"Well, get him oot o' here right now," Sadie said.

"Well, we canny use the wheelchair again," Erchie said, "every polis in Glesca wull be lookin' for wan and a hauf men pushin' a wheelchair. We've still got Bunty's auld pram?"

"He wull never fit in that," Sadie said.

"Well we canny cairry him doon the street in that position," Erchie said, thinking hard.

"Ah've seen you gettin' cairried hame many a time in that position," Sadie said.

"Never in broad daylight, Sadie," Erchie said.

"Y'know, Erchie, Ah'm surprised they ever gave you a joab in

Shakutis. No' efter how ye filled that application form in," Sadie said.

"Whit dae ye mean?" Erchie asked.

"At the question ' whit religion ur ye?' You put doon *racist*."

"Ah put doon RC," Erchie protested.

"Ay, an *a* in the middle and *ist* at the end," Sadie said.

"Well, Ah believe in bein' honest," Erchie said, "Besides they would've fun' oot everytime Ah stuck ma tongue oot at them – especially that wee Nyaff."

"This is a' very well," Sadie said, "But whit ur ye gonny dae aboot him," she nodded towards the window.

"It's jist a pity we hivnae got a travois," Tyrone said.

Sadie and Erchie glanced at each other. Had Tyrone been chewing a dictionary?

"Every hoose should hiv wan," Erchie said.

"It would've solved oor problem," Tyrone said.

"Ah was thinkin' that masel'," Erchie said. "There's jist wan other problem."

"Whit's that?" Tyrone said.

"Whit is it?" Erchie said.

"It's wan o' them Indian things ye see in the cowboy films, know whit Ah mean? Ye've seen travois millions o' times."

Tyrone was delighted that he knew something that Erchie did not.

"Of coorse Ah know whit ye mean," Erchie sniped. "Ye don't think for a minute that *you* know mair than me, dae ye? "Ah merely forgot for a minute aboot travois."

"Whit is it, then?" Tyrone said.

"It's – er – wan o' them things used by the Indians," he said.

"Whit things?"

"Wan o' them things we hivnae got," Erchie said. "Besides, when did you become an expert on Rid Indians?"

"Ah jist took it a' in. Ah know a loat o' Indian words an' that."

"Like whit?" Erchie asked.

Tyrone cleared his throat. "How," he said, " 'White man speak with forked tongue'. Ah know a' the big chiefs and hiv ma favourites."

"Dae ye like Cochise?"

"Ah like it oan crackers," Tyrone said.

97

"Ye're talkin' a loat o' rubbish as usual," Erchie said, mimicking. " 'Ah like it oan crackers'."

"Right," Tyrone said, "a travois would hiv been jist the thing, wouldn't it?"

"Ah would say 'aye' if Ah knew whit ye wur talkin' aboot," Erchie said.

"A Travois – ye've seen the Indians usin' when wan o' them gets shot and he fa's aff his hoarse and is lyin' wounded. Then wan o' his pals rides up, sees him lyin' there in agony and immediately he yells oot 'Right, boys, get um Travois for Wullie who is wounded'. So, they get two big poles and an auld door if there's wan lyin' around and the attach the poles tae the door then attach them tae a hoarse and lay Wullie oan tap and gee-up alang the trail." Tyrone felt elated.

"Right, Sadie, you take the hinges aff that door and get a couple o' yer pulley poles and Ah'll go oot n' look for a hoarse."

"That's how it's done," Tyrone said.

"Whit if they canny, by some quirk of fate, find an auld door lyin' oot there in the desert – whit dae they dae then?" Erchie asked quizzically.

"They shoot a sojer and stick the poles through the erms of his tunic nae bother," Tyrone said, smiling.

"Ah was jist testin' ye, Tyrone," Erchie said. "Ah knew whit wan o' them travoirs was a' the time. Sadie, forget takin' the hinges aff the door n we'll no bother shootin' a sojer either. And there's no' many hoarses aboot thesedays. And, besides, Ah think we would look awfu' consp – cons – conscriptuous goin' doon Sauchiehall Street like Sittin' Bill and Crazy Hoarse."

"We could pluck a chicken and stick its feathers in oor heid," Tyrone volunteered.

"Naw, naw," Erchie said, "Geronimo an' them didnae hiv chicken feathers in their heids. Geronimo, Chief Crazy Horse and Chief Sittin' Bull rode intae battle wearing eagle feathers. Only wan chief didnae. He wore a motor bike helmet."

"Whit was his name?" Tyrone asked.

"Chief Bald Eagle," Erchie said.

After much discussion it was decided that the "windae cleaner" should be strapped into the rear saddle of Tyrone's father's old tandem pedal cycle. Their guest was the proper shape and the dynamic duo could not see any problems.

This was done and the pair set off with Tyrone riding the tandem and Erchie following behind on his old bike. Stopped at the traffic lights, at High Street and George Street, a police car had pulled up alongside of Tyrone.

"No' oaften ye se a tandem these days," one of the policemen remarked to his partner.

"Look at them teeth!" his mate said. "Either he's enjoyin' the wind oan his face or he's sittin' oan a nail."

"Does he look familiar tae you?" the other asked.

"Naw, he looks like a foreigner," his partner said. "Could be Welsh or somethin'."

"How can ye tell?"

"He's got leak at his nose," his mate said and the lights changed. The patrol speeded off with a scream of tyres and Tyrone sighed a long sigh. Erchie whistled and stared at the sky. Tyrone went past the traffic lights at George Square and pulled into the side with Erchie right behind him.

"Whit's up?" Erchie called.

"Ah canny go oan, Erchie," Tyrone said. "That polis car unhinged me so it did."

"You've always been aff yer hinges," Erchie said.

"How an we get away wi' this,eh?" Tyrone whimpered. "Ah mean his legs urnae movin'. He jist sits there wi' a face like Dalbeth Cemetery. Somebody's bound tae notice. Dae we really hiv tae take him a' the wey tae the Art Galleries? Ah mean we jist want tae dump him."

Tyrone had a point, Erchie thought. The longer they had the Samurai in their possession their chances of being caught the greater.

"Right!" he said at last, making up his mind. "We'll sit him oan wan o' the seats in the Square – come on'."

They carried the Samurai Warrior into the Square and placed him on one of the public benches. Both walked nonchalantly away, now and again turning to see there was no hassle. The Warrior sat alone and erect looking straight ahead and grinning broadly,

"Ye'd better phone Sadie oan yer mobile an' tell her everythin's a'right noo."

"Aye, right enough," Erchie said. "She'll be annoyed if she thinks we've been spotted by the polis."

"In case they arrest ye?" Tyrone asked.

"In case they don't," Erchie laughed.

Erchie called Sadie and told her he and Tyrone were clear and that Tojo was sitting comfortably on a bench in George Square. He could almost hear Sadie doing cartwheels. Not only had she got rid of an unwanted guest but had gained a window. She could even hing oot' if she wanted to, although that was a dying art.

The pair mounted their bikes and rode off giving one last backward glance at their old friend. People walked past the sitting figure with barely a look. He was just another Japanese tourist. Only one person took any notice of the solitary figure sitting in the chilly afternoon. Warmth for this foreign gentleman sitting alone, baring his teeth, was too much for this slightly inebriated Glaswegian. Like all Glaswegians, his heart swelled with compassion at the sight of a lonely figure and a foreigner to boot. Slowly and with a staggering gait the wee man made his way over to the bench and flopped down beside the still figure.

"How's it gaun, China?" he said and chuckled. "Heh-heh – get it? – *China* – heh-heh. – Hey, an whit've you been drinkin' – liquid stookie? Ah've heard o'a stiff drink but you're the first wan Ah've seen wi' wan. Ur ye cauld, son, ye're freezin' – and Ah don't know whit the hell ye've got tae smile aboot. Well, it's been nice meetin' ye, Jimmy." The drunk went on, "Ah'm goin' away hame noo tae frozen face jist like yours only withoot the teeth. So, keep smilin' as long as ye've got the teeth tae smile wi'. For I might no' hiv mine before this night is oot." And with a final cheery wave the man staggered off.

Erchie and Tyrone, pleased with their work, stopped at the *Two Haufs* hostelry, in the Gallowgate.

Erchie made for a table in the corner after despatching Tyrone to the bar with an order for two pints of McEwans Heavy and with the command not to get any of that 'German muck'.

Tyrone duly obliged and staggered back to the table.

"Cheers," they toasted, with clinking glasses.

"Well, that was a good day's work, eh?" Tyrone said.

"It's good for tae get rid of auld Tojo. Sadie wull be pleased for tae get rid o' that Jap rubbish."

"It's a shame that you're like that," Tyrone said. "Hiv ye always been a racist, Erchie?" Tyrone looked interested.

"No' always, Tyrone," Erchie said. "Weans urnae racist it's only as ye get aulder ye become a racist. Ah didnae start aff as wan."

"Whit age wur ye when ye became wan?" Tyrone asked.

"Four," Erchie said, taking a sip of his beer.

"Whit made that happen, then?" Tyrone asked.

"It wis Christmas and ma maw proamised for tae take me and ma wee sister tae Fraser's for to see Santa Claus. Ah was really lookin' forward tae it. Then, the night before we wur due tae go, she was washin' me at the sink an' discovered wee red spots a' ower me. An' that was that – nae Santa for me."

"Whit was it, Erchie – Chicken pox?" Tyrone asked.

"You've got chickens on the brain," Erchie snapped. "Chicken feathers – chicken pox. It was *measles* Tyrone, *measles*." Erchie was bitter.

"So how should that make ye a racist, then?" Tyrone asked.

"It was *German* measles," Erchie said angrily. "Then, when Ah was six Ah took *Asian* 'flu and it jist esculumated frae there, *Dehli Belly – Yella Fever*. Ah've had them a'. Noo, ye can see ma point." Erchie spat out the words.

"Ye canny go by that, Erchie," Tyrone said, "That shouldnae make ye a racist. Ah mean, ma da' had green fingers but he didnae become a Celtic supporter know whit Ah mean?"

"Ach, shut yer face ya wee imbecile," Erchie said.

Tyrone let Erchie's insults run off his back. He knew he did not mean them and was just venting his anger on the person nearest to him. The pair enjoyed the hospitality of the *Two Haufs* hostelry for the next couple of hours. As they left, Erchie suggested they ride back to George Square and see if their 'freen' was still there. It took just a few minutes to ride the couple of miles. And they were overjoyed to see the bench empty.

The pair dismounted and sat on the vacant bench and swept their eyes over the red asphalted square to see if anyone was carrying their 'freen' off.

Some office workers, out for their lunch break, hurried across the square, some going into Greggs for their made-up sandwiches, others into the *Counting House* bar and restaurant for a

101

full meal. Most of the other activity was due to the busy, scavenager pigeons. Some Japanese tourists pointed cameras at the impressive City Chambers and at each other in front of the cenotaph which was guarded by two proud stone lions.

"Noo, look at them Jap tourists," Tyrone said. "They's jist like anybody else – daein' whit everybody does when they're on hoaliday – does that no' make ye see how daft it is for tae be racist?"

"Ur you some kinda nut?" Erchie said.

"We ur a' Joack Thamson's bairns, Erchie," Tyrone said. "D'ye believe in God?"

"He's got nuthin' tae dae wi' it," Erchie growled." And, besides Ah do *nut* believe in him. Sadie does, Ah don't."

"Whit colour dae ye think *He* is?" Tyrone asked.

"Ah said Ah didnae believe in him, for God's sake, ur ye deef?" Erchie snapped.

"Naw, but jist think aboot it, Erchie," Tyrone said. "God made us a' every wan o' us. So, he's got nae favourites, right! Jist imagine a field fuull o' flooers a' the wan colour say, rid or yella or broon or green. Noo, that widnae be as nice as a field fuull o' a' different colours, wid it? See whit Ah mean? When the Big Man made the world *He* reckoned that it wid be mair beautiful wi' a loat o' different coloura, aye?"

Erchie narrowed his eyes and looked, quizzically, at Tyrone. "Hiv you been readin' the *War Cry* again?" he asked suspiciously.

"Naw, dae ye no' see whit Ah mean?" Tyrone said.

"Ah see yer analagreba," Erchie said. "Maybe *He* is colour blind"

"It's *you* that's colour blind, Erchie," Tyrone said bravely.

Normally Erchie would have flattened Tyrone but the wee man's words struck a chord and Erchie felt uncomfortable . For once he found himself tongue-tied. You do not know what philosophers you will meet during the day. Erchie cleared his throat.

Erchie heard the sound of laughter as he put his key in the lock. He looked at Tyrone who shrugged. The pair were taken aback as they entered the living room. Sitting on the easy chair was the

Samurai Warrior. And facing him Mr Nagazumi sat polishing his glasses and chuckling loudly.

"Whi – whit's this?" Erchie demanded.

" Ah, Honourable Erchie," Nagazumi said, "look we have our Samurai Warrior back."

"Ah can see that, "Erchie said, "bu – bu —"

"Do not you recognise him, eh?" Nagazumi went on. "Very much like honourable window cleaner, no?"

"There *is* a wee resemblance," Tyrone said.

"You shut yer face, you," Erchie sniped, adding, "Ah don't see it. The windae cleaner looked mair like the wee Nyaff your horrible nephew."

"Ah, honourable nephew no longer employed in Shakutis. I no like his methods. He now work in sushi restaurant in Argyle Street."

" It's aboot time you saw throught that wee Nyaff. Whit wull yer sister say?"

"No' like her either. She a racist," Nagazumi said.

"How can she be a racist," Erchie said, "she's no' wan o' us?"

"She think you all look the same," Nagazumi said.

"Only when we're headin' for Parkheid or Ibrox," Erchie said. "But where did ye find Tojo, here?"

"Him sitting on bench in beautiful George Square along with pigeons. Then I get a phone call from a pigeon who talks."

"Pigeons canny talk, Mr Nagazumi," Tyrone said.

"They talk my language," Nagazumi said.

"Japanese?" Tyrone asked.

"Pigeon English," Nagazumi laughed.

"So, whit is he daein' here, in this hoose?" Erchie asked.

"I pick him up from his bench and thought he might like to visit honourable hoose where he been stayin' before going back to be re-acquainted with honourable cuddy at Art Galleries." Nagazumi laughed heartily and removing his glasses wiped his eyes.

"Ye mean you knew a' the time that oor windae cleaner wis your Samurai Warrior?" Erchie gasped.

"Honourable eyes bad but no' *that* bad," Nagazumi said. "But sometimes it is better to turn a blind eye and see if dishonourable culprit will show remorse – especially when one admires the honesty and devotion in a good lady's pleading eyes."

Erchie looked at Sadie who smiled. A sudden knock on the door made Tyrone jump. Sadie answered and there were muffled voices from the lobby. Then Sadie entered with Detective Inspector McSponger.

"Everything a'right, Mr Nagazumi?" the Inspector asked.

"Everything fine, Charlie," Nagazumi said.

"*Charlie?*" Erchie cried. "His name is Hamish McSponger, the pride o' the Strathclyde polis department."

"No, no," Nagazumi chuckled. "This is Charlie Rodger, actor with honourable Japanese State Theatre Company."

"*Him?* How can he be a Jap actor? He's got a face like a bucket o' whitewash."

"Honourable Theatre company need actors to play Western roles."

"Ye mean he plays parts like Billy the Kid an' that?" Tyrone said in awe.

"Don't be stupit," Erchie said. "He means he plays parts that call for men that come frae oor side o' the world."

"Whit side is that, Erchie?" Tyrone asked.

"The other side frae theirs," Erchie snapped.

"I suspect you all the time," Nagazumi said, "but I admire loyalty of honourable Missy Sadie. This is a treasure in life. To have such devotion. So, I did not want to spoil it for her. Also want to see if you contrite and return honourable Warrior by yourself."

"Ah helped him," Tyrone said.

"You good wee man – daft, but good," Nagazumi said.

"And you," he said, to Erchie, "you get your joab back – thanks to honourable wife."

"Well, honourable wife and me fight a' the time," Erchie said.

"All married couple fight," Nagazumi said.

"No' wi' swords, they don't," Erchie said.

"Ach, away ye go ya skallywag," Sadie said, laughing.

"Jist promise me the next time ye kiss me ye'll no' put yer Dracula teeth in," Erchie laughed, giving Sadie an affectionate nudge in the ribs. "An' Ah'm no' goin' back if that wee Nyaff . . ."

"I told you honourable nephew sacked and working in sushi restaurant," Mr Nagazuni said.

"Excuse me, Mr Nagazumi," Charlie Rodgers interrupted, "is it all right if I go? We are busy rehearsing the er – the er – Scottish Play."

"Whit's the 'Scottish Play'?" Erchie asked, drawing down his eyebrows.

"Every actor knows that," Sadie said, " but it's supposed to be unlucky for them to say the proper title so they jist call it the 'Scottish Play'."

"Ah know whit the right title o' the Scottish Play is an' Ah can say it 'cos Ah'm no' an actor," Tyrone said eagerly.

"You're no' even a human bein'," Erchie said."So, tell us. Whit *is* the right name for the Scottish Play, eh?

"*The Steamie*," Tyrone said with a smug expression.

"Away ye go, "Sadie said, "It's *Macbeth*."

"Ah knew that a' the time. Ah was jist testin' gormeless, here." Erchie stated.

"Well, if you two gentlemen would take honourable Samurai down to my car I will re-unite him with his honourable hoarse," Nagazumi said.

"Nae bother," Erchie said, "C'mon, Ty you grab that leg." The two men manhandled the Warrior out of the door and out to the large Rolls Bentley. Mr Nagazumi turned at the door and taking Sadie's hand, bowed and kissed it.

"Honourable Sadie, you keep card I gave you in case I can ever be of assistance to you. And thank you for important telephone call saying where honourable Samurai was located."

"Thanks for gien' Erchie his joab back, Mr Nagazumi," Sadie said, "He's no' really a bad man – foolish at times, that's a'."

"He a lucky man to have such a lovely, understanding wife," Nagazumi said and bowing once more left.

Erchie and Tyrone came back puffing and panting.

"Geez, he's heavy, eh,?" Erchie said. Tyrone made an excuse saying he would have to go and see if everything was all right next door. He borrowed Erchie's bicycle pump and left.

"Well, hen, that's that!" Erchie said.

Sadie took his hand and, squeezing it affectionately, said. "Don't let Mr Nagazumi doon, Erchie. If ye let *him* doon, ye're lettin' *me* doon. Ye've got another chance."

"Aye, and it's thanks tae you tae," Erchie said, embarrassingly pecking her cheek.

"Ye must admit that yer recent acitivities hiv been stupid tae say the least," Sadie said.

"Only because Ah didnae get away wi' them, hen," Erchie said.

"Proamise me wan thing, Erchie," Sadie said, with a pleading look in her eye. "Proamise ye'll stoap a' this racist rubbish. We've a' got tae live the gether and we ur a' Joac . . ."

"Ah know," Erchie interrupted, "we're a' Joack Campbell's bairns."

"*Tamson's*," Sadie corrected.

"Aye, him an' a'," Erchie said.

"D'ye proamise, then? Nae mair racist cairry oan?" Sadie repeated.

"Cross ma hert," Erchie said, crossing his heart. "If Ah break ma proamise, Ah'll gie up ma favourite hobby."

"Drinkin'?" Sadie asked.

"Fitba'," Erchie said quickly, "and take up origami."

"That a proamise?" Sadie said. "Nae mair racist talk?"

"As God's ma judge," Erchie said.

Bunty's bedroom door flew open and she emerged looking radiant in full Geisha costume and jet-black wig. Her face chalk white.

"How dae Ah look?" she purred, taking up a Geisha dancing pose.

"Aw, naw! It's Madame Butterfly. Geisha a break, hen!" Erchie gasped, "Look – look at her coupon it's whiter than ma bank book. She's dead like Michael Jackson."

"Ye look lovely, hen," Sadie said. "Aff tae yer fancy dress party? Hiv a rerr terr and watch how ye go."

"Ah don't know how they Geishas could walk never mind run wearin' this gear," Bunty said, shuffling.

"That was the idea," Erchie said.

Suddenly there was a loud knock on the door.

"Oh, that'll be ma date," Bunty said, excitedly.

"Ah'll get it," Sadie said, answering the door.

Adolph strutted in a Hitler look-a-like, complete with postage stamp black moustache. He clicked his heels and gave the Nazi salute.

"Heil me," he said.

"Ah telt you we wur finished," Bunty cried. "Get away, Ah never want tae see you again."

Adolph started to protest but Erchie shoved him through the door.

"You heard her noo, beat it – oot – oot."

Adolph took the hint and hurried away protesting vehemently.

"Ye did the right thing there, hen," Erchie said. Within minutes there was another knock at the door.

"That'll be Angus," Bunty said, smiling.

"Angus? Aye, that's mair like it, hen," Echie said.

"Ah'll get it," Sadie said, answering the door. Angus entered and bowed.

Erchie exploded and pointing a shaking finger at Bunty's date, bawled, "It's *him*...it's *him*...it's the *Wee Nyaff* . . ."

He rushed past Angus and out into the street, running down the street yelling, "Adolph come back – Adolph come back, son – come back . . ."

Sadie turned and looked at Bunty. She nodded towards the sideboard.

"Fetch me the scissors frae the tap drawer, hen," Sadie said, "and haun' me that auld *Daily Record*. Yer faither's takin' up a new hobby."

LINDSAY PUBLICATIONS
PO BOX 812 GLASGOW G14 9NP
TEL/FAX 0141 569 6060
ISBN Prefix 1 898169

1 898169 00 4	Scottish Home Baking	£4.95
01 2	Highland Dancing	£10.00
03 9	Scottish Home Cooking	£4.95
05 5	Taste of Scotland	£8.99
06 3	Homecraft	£3.99
07 1	Robert Burns	£4.99
08 x	Glasgow's River	£9.99
09 8	Savour of Ireland	£9.99
10 1	Surgeon's Apprentice	£4.99
11 x	Lines Around the City	£10.99
12 8	Savour of Scotland	£9.99
13 6	Still a Bigot	£4.99
14 4	Happy Landings	£4.99
15 2	Twisted Knickers & Stolen Scones	£9.99
16 0	Away with the Ferries	£9.99
17 9	Will I be Called an Author?	£7.99
18 7	Topsy & Tim aig an Fhaiclair	£4.99
19 5	T & T aig an Dotair	£4.99
20 9	T & T agus na Smaladairean	£4.99
21 7	T & T agus na Polis	£4.99
22 5	Laughing Matters	£8.99
23 3	A Wheen O' Blethers	£8.99
24 1	Oot the Windae	£7.99
25 x	Oor Hoose	£4.99
26 8	Full Cycle	£9.99
27.6	The Cardinal	£9.99
28 4	Nippon Aboot	£4.99